MASKS

Stella had thought she was surrounded by love . . . by safety . . . here in her own country . . . with her own people. . . .

Now she saw every smiling face as a mask . . . her sympathetic, sophisticated friends . . . the concerned government officials . . . the man who had come back from the grave to claim her as his bride. . . .

All were players in a sinister charade . . . and Stella had been cast in the role of victim. . . .

You will never forget
the shock of discovery in—
HUNTER IN THE SHADOWS

"Genuine power and individuality."
—THE NEW YORK TIMES

HUNTER IN THE SHADOWS

✳✳✳✳✳✳✳✳✳✳✳✳✳✳✳✳✳✳✳✳✳✳✳✳✳✳✳✳✳✳✳✳

JENNIE MELVILLE

A DELL BOOK

Published by
DELL PUBLISHING CO., INC.
750 Third Avenue
New York, New York 10017

Dell ® TM 681510, Dell Publishing Co., Inc.
Reprinted by arrangement with
David McKay, Inc.
New York, New York

Printed in the U.S.A.
First Dell printing—March 1971

CHAPTER ONE

The interrogator, sitting in a quiet dark room, high above the river, said, "By all means let us hear everything she has to say. It may be interesting."

The man he was speaking to said, "It can hardly fail to be that."

"By interesting, I mean informative, useful to us."

"Perhaps. She was very careful."

"And how did you get this script?"

The other smiled. "*She* wrote it down. Oh, she wants to tell the story. A natural impulse. But there is someone in contact with her."

"We have continued to watch her?"

"Naturally."

"Naturally." He nodded affirmation.

The other said, "I always find it so interesting to listen to people living through episodes like this."

"Cool bastard!"

He knocked at the door and when I opened it he said he was my husband, but his ten years in the grave could not have changed my husband that much and anyway we didn't speak the same language. He was tall (my husband had been tall) with brown hair and a deep tan and the sort of muscles to go with a deep tan. In his forties, you'd say, forty at the most. Age difficult to assess. He looked both powerful and gentle. I thought I wouldn't trust the gentleness just yet.

No, he wasn't my husband. He had a long way to go before he resembled my husband. It was just some fancy threat.

Of course, he wasn't the first, the only one to come

calling. He might be regarded as more or less the cul-
mination. The end of a procession.

First, there was the one who said he was an old
friend of my mother's and had known her as a young
married woman. He was small and plump and friendly
and reminded me of my mother who was also small
and plump and friendly. Less friendly perhaps as she
grew older. He came in and had tea, which he took
with a great deal of sugar, also like my mother. He
talked with feeling of my mother, all the time with his
eyes wandering round my sitting room. He seemed to
know a lot of detail about mother as a young woman
and he certainly knew her face. He picked it out in a
group photograph. Even pointing to one that he said
was his own. "That's me, Willy," he said, with his
finger on one smiling young face among all the friends
on a picnic. So he was Willy. Or else he'd done his
homework.

Then there was the man who said he was an art
dealer and was interested in a painting my husband
had left me. Anything my husband left me, I value. I
did not let him in. Instead, I went and looked at the
painting. This is an oil painting of a country scene
with a few seated figures and a ruin. It is small and
dark, yet glows. I love it. However it is not a lost
Giorgione or anything like that. It is simply a small
dark oil painting of a country scene. My husband
bought it because he thought it was the site of a primi-
tive civilisation which he wanted to excavate. I love it
because he bought it.

After him was the woman who came to ask my advice. I thought at first she'd come to take my money,
she had such a firm fierce way with her. But no, she
only wanted my views on living in this district. She
was thinking of moving in and wanted me to tell her
what it was like. I said it was fine, lovely, a little run-
down like a lot of places now, near the bridge, but
too far to walk anywhere in the city, and quiet. I
was surprised because she looked more a woman for

the suburbs, for one of those nice, American-style houses they are building out there now, or a flat in one of the new massive blocks which look as though they could be and might have to be defended against a tank attack. "You're lovely and high up here," she said, moving over to my window and looking out. "What a nice place you've got." She seemed to have an instinctive grasp of the lay-out; she took everything in. When she left I felt she knew my pulse rate and temperature as well. But she never moved in and, so far, I've not seen her again.

So you see the man at the door now was only one in a queue. But he had his foot in the door and was in the house before I could stop him.

I live in a small, very reasonably priced flat high on the top of my building. Underneath me is a doctor, an apprentice gynaecologist in a big hospital. Beneath the doctor is a hairdresser. She isn't seen much; she works hard, long hours. There are several floors beneath them, but the people here are conservative and quiet. I know their names and nod but that's the end. One is a teacher, I think, and another a civil servant. That's what they look like. An elderly couple have the ground floor flat. I often speak to them at their open window. She grows lovely geraniums and has given me a cutting. You can see that none of us are rich. But the building has a little elegance left over from the old days and on my top floor where I can look down on the roof tops and at the church at the corner I am happy. It's an oddly shaped curving street with all the buildings abutting on each other so that you always look at an angle. Round a characteristic half curve, half angle is the handsome Romanesque church. Only part of it is visible from my end of the street but from my window I can see all the curves and rotundas of the roof. There are two other old buildings cut up into apartments in the street, all equally quiet, but owing to the doctor and the school teacher and also me, we in our house are known locally as 'the intellectuals'. At the end of the street is a noisy main road and just around the corner another church. So we are well provided with churches, fine buildings both of them. Not that anyone ever goes in them much except a few old women and visitors. I go in myself occasionally and walk around in a surprised kind of way, willing to say a prayer but not quite sure who's at home to say it to.

Some people can manage without prayer. I didn't think I could. But it's not easy to say prayers in our generation, to know who to say them to or what to say. I was not twenty when I married thirteen years ago; I have ash blonde hair which the new straight styles suit. In some ways I am younger than my years, in others older.

I live alone except for my cat, fairly happy and quite absorbed in my work which wins me the name of 'intellectual'. For the last eight years I have been one of a team engaged in making children's films for television. They are very popular and we export a lot as well. We pat ourselves on the back with every success and say how clever we are to earn foreign money, but the truth is we love what we create and do it with joy. I'm as bad as anyone and I believe I'm supposed to be the one with the business head in our team. At the moment we are making a film based on an old folk story, itself based upon a fragment of real history, and I have done the research for it. Yes, I *am* an intellectual, you see.

In my group at college I didn't stand out as the intellectual one. We all thought we were that. Took it for granted, it was the basis of our whole life, naturally we were intellectuals. What were we doing at university else? Anne, Catherine, Xandra and me. We were charming little snobs. Even me, and heaven knows I had no reason to be. The other girls' families were nothing special, looked at from many points of view, but they were comfortably placed. They knew where they were in the world. They were my friends, Anne, Catherine and Xandra, but I was not quite one of them. I was not altogether of their blood (of course, it was not noticeable, almost forgotten—but perhaps not quite overlooked?) and I had had a Jewish grandmother. No, we were close friends, truly loved each other, or so I think, but I was not quite like them and they had a number of little ways of letting me know it. They could give me a special smile, an indulgent shrug or sometimes just a long careful explanation. As a child and as a young girl growing up in this circle (we all four went to the same school) I longed to be totally and absolutely acceptable. I never seemed to quite catch up with them. They were always cutting their hair when I was just starting to grow mine, they knew first when it was time to slim and lose weight, and they knew what subjects to choose first year at university. It was no comfort to me then that on the whole I got the best marks.

This longing to be one of them marked my growing up. I dreamed about it but it never seemed to happen. But as the years went on I worked hard, made my career, got married and ceased to think about it. And that, I suppose, was when it came about.

But I have gone on seeing Anne and Catherine and Xandra, they are still my friends, and strangely enough don't seem to notice that they have lost any domination over me. Perhaps they never realised they had it, after all. Anne is married but lives sometimes with her husband and sometimes apart from him. She is a brilliant doctor and he is a brilliant scientist. It wasn't a marriage that was ever going to work, but they keep on trying. Catherine has no career but works all the same because she needs the money; she and her husband let Catherine's mother look after their only child while they both work. I don't know why more didn't happen to Catherine, she was so very pretty, she ought to have had a big life of it. Yet she's happy. I swear she's happy. Xandra comes and goes in our life like a linnet. She's an actress. Funny way to end up for her

who was going to be a historian, but she's successful
and has even been to America. Looking back I can't remember how or why Xandra became an actress, can't
put my finger on any moment when we looked at each
other and said Xandra will act, Xandra will be a star.
It just seemed to come about. Anyway it's turned out
very useful for us, because she brings us back presents
of scent and foreign clothes from her tours.

I see more of Xandra than the others because our
worlds meet. She acts; I have to do with actors. I've
been thinking of getting her to act the part of the
Princess in our new production; she'd take the part
of the Princess beautifully. But the shape of the film
hasn't been settled yet. So far we have used only
puppets. Now I want us to try using real actors. But
I don't know. We've been successful so far in the
style we've created, perhaps it would be wrong to
change. Whenever I say to Xandra, "Oh how funny it
is to think of you as an actress," she answers, "And
whoever else would have thought you'd be in the business either, even making films for toddlers, you that
was going to be the great woman politician." And then
we both laugh. It's lucky we can laugh when we both
know that life changes so many things. "I'm not
political really," I say. "You better not be," says
Xandra, rolling her great blue eyes. She's not a come-
dian, by the way, not on the stage anyway. Mother
Courage was her last role. She's in training now for
Lady Macbeth. They hope to take the production to
Warsaw, Moscow and New York. Xandra says she'd
prefer Paris. French scent is better than Russian scent.

When I married I meant to give up work, but being
married is expensive even if your husband is a widower
who has lots of furniture and pots and pans so I kept
on for a while. Then, when he went on his famous trip
to do his long looked-for dig to discover the civilisation
older than the Hittites and first was a long time coming
back and then never came back at all, I was glad to
work.

"I don't understand why you don't remarry," said my stepdaughter Justine one night over coffee. She doesn't live with me, she has her own place to live. When she's in it. She works so hard. In this she is her father's child. Mine a little too, I hope, because I really brought her up.

"You sound as though you're cross with me for not."

"I am a little. You're young still. Pretty. You ought to marry. Why don't you?"

"I don't know. I've never wanted to again. Yes, I suppose it's as simple as that." I smiled at her. A little hard to explain to your stepdaughter exactly how and in what way you loved her father and how this love was still strong in you. "For a long while, of course, I couldn't accept that he was dead."

"No. It was the same with me."

"How much can you remember your father? You were only a young girl."

"Well, not so young. And I remember many things. I remember he was kind, but not particularly patient."

I laughed. "Very impatient often. Yet sometimes so patient it was unbelievable."

"He had a quick temper. He was loving. He loved me, and you, anyway. I suppose he loved my mother. Of course I don't remember that. She died before I remember anything."

"What a lot of sadness you've had," I said, and she was so young. Who had really made Justine what she was? Good and true. Perhaps she'd done it herself.

"So he had a lot of love in him," she went on. "I remember that. But not his physical appearance. Isn't it strange? I don't remember what he looked like."

"In memory," I said sadly, "that always goes first."

"I've seen photographs, of course. But now, I wouldn't know him if I saw him."

It was a sad thing for her to say in the light of later events. Justine has always been very sensitive, sometimes appearing to know things before they happened. But neither of us felt anything of a threat then.

"I had a letter from an old school friend of your father's the other day," I said. "Wasn't it strange? He didn't seem to know he was dead." The letter had worried me somewhat. I wasn't quite normal in my reactions to my husband's death and that was the truth.

I had told Justine about the letter from my husband's old school friend. I hadn't told her that an unknown voice had called for him on the telephone. A letter. A 'phone call. And today, finally, the most unnerving of all, as if he was still alive, a receipted bill had come for him. It was a bill from the Mavian Travel Agency for a railway ticket, destination unspecified. In my nightmare, it might seem he was travelling back.

"But that's the thing about my father, I suppose," she said. "He's dead but we've never buried him. And that's what keeps you from remarrying and keeps me with my nose to my work. All the time I'm thinking that if he came back I'd want to turn round and say 'Look, this is what I've achieved'."

"But that's not the only reason you work so hard."

"No. No, it absorbs me by its very nature."

She was so lovely, my beautiful Justine. And so vulnerable. Once physicists were the vulnerable ones among scientists, subject to all sorts of pressures, known and unknown, but events have moved on and now it is a certain sort of biochemist. And it was in this field that Justine excelled. The work she did there was sensitive and terrible. She never spoke of it and I only guessed the way her work was moving from her silences.

She didn't go on talking then, just smiled and said goodbye. I was alone again.

My old cat, tawny and grey, dragged himself to the window, then leapt, with surprising ease, to the sunny patch on the sill and went to sleep among the geraniums. I know that if you go down to the road and cross to the other side you can look up and see him sleeping there. He no longer has a name or even a character, he is so old; he belonged to my husband and before him to someone else. Now he belongs just to the flat and himself.

When my caller appeared at my door I thought at first he had come for Justine. There *was* something familiar about him and without knowing why I connected it with Justine. He stood for a moment looking friendly and hopeful. Then he made his surprising announcement which my mind is still reluctant to put into words.

"Stella," he said, putting out his hands.

I have this ridiculous name. My father loved the stars. He read a passage about them to himself every day like someone else might read from the Bible. But he shouldn't have called me Stella. It's always made people expect more from me than I have to offer. Stella is a name for a girl who is going to come to a happy ending, and somehow I have never felt that was me.

"Yes, I'm Stella," I answered. I still held the door open with one hand. He could see past me into the little square hall and then beyond that to the living room with the open windows and the geraniums. The old cat came and stood in the hall and stared at us.

"Atabi," he cried out. Yes, that had been the old cat's name. Atabi, the striped one. "You've still got Atabi. He's still alive."

"Who are you?" I said.

"Stella, I'm your husband. Aren't you going to let me in?"

He pushed past me gently into the hall, then he walked confidently into the living room. He knew his way around but then he would do. His forerunners had had a good look round for him.

"I know it's been a long, long while; nearly ten years, but still . . ."

"It's more than ten years," I said. "You've been *dead*."

"Stella, let me explain."

"You're not my husband. Of course, you're not my husband. You don't even look like him." And I walked quickly to the window and opened it a little more (although it was a hot evening and it was already grey) as if I could blow away his ghost.

"Are you sure I don't look like him?"

"Yes." I was indignant. "He was about your height and had the same sort of bones but there's no genuine resemblance at all."

"Ten years is a long time."

"You're thinner than him."

"I was ill. For a long time."

"Ah, so that's how you're going to explain it. Explain why you never came back and let us all think you were lost in that wild place. Lost and dead. You were ill. Well, yes, I heard you were ill. Now you're going to say you lost your memory."

"No. Not my memory. Lost my power of movement."

"Yes, you'd have to produce some sort of answer. Even an unbelievable one. What sort of a fool do you think I am? What sort of a wife do you think I was?"

"A very loving one, Stella."

There was absolute dead silence. I felt myself go white.

He saw it too and put his arm out, but I steadied myself.

Those words meant something to me. They had formed a small joke. "I'm not an efficient wife," I used to say, "but I'm a loving one." They came to be a joke we used between us when we wished to express much more than we knew how to say.

It was cruel and wicked of him, if he had come to know of this joke, to use these words.

"What is it you want? Why have you come here?" They were silly, silly words but I felt I had to utter them. If this had been a play for my puppets I would have written them better dialogue.

"I want to come in."

He was in. I didn't answer. I looked towards the telephone.

"I'll telephone the police."

"No." He looked at me. "You won't do that."

It was stupid. I know the police are often good simple men, still I did not want to call them. I should grow out of this attitude of being frightened of the police, of thinking of them as enemies, but it isn't easy. Anyway some of them I suspect are still enemies. In their hearts. Even policemen of that sort have hearts. That, alas, is the trouble, because where the rest of us spread our love out (love homes, friends, family, truth, God) men like them have concentrated their love on one or two objects; it might be themselves or their country or even just their job, and in their hard tight-packed little hearts they have no room to spare. No, I didn't want to meet a policeman like that.

"I'm not frightened," I said defiantly. "I'm angry. Get out."

He didn't make any move to go. Instead he moved further into the room. I saw then that he moved as if he was tired. He had a small bag with him and this he placed on a chair.

I took a step towards the door. Hurriedly I was running over who was in the building. It was early evening, everyone would be home getting ready to eat.

The people on the ground floor were old and fragile. And even if they were not, terrible things had already taken place in their life; they no longer even saw their daughter, she was gone, perhaps from this world, certainly from their lives. I couldn't involve them in anything else.

What about the school teacher and the civil servants underneath? I could go to the door and shout, "Help," and they'd come running, enjoy it probably, they had dull lives and were bored with them.

But then when they got there, what then? Supposing

he said: "I am her husband." What would they do? Mutter and mumble apologetically and crawl away; that's what they might do.

And then, when they got downstairs and thought about it, wouldn't they get very nervous indeed and decide that the best thing for them to do as school teachers and civil servants was to keep right out of it? No one wanted to end up in a police station or even in a cell just because they'd seen the wrong person at the wrong time. Did I have a right to make cowards of them?

I drew back.

"No," he said, watching me, and giving a nod. "No help from there."

I thought for a moment about the hairdresser who had once chased three hoodlums out of her shop, but then I remembered she was away for the night. She had a married daughter living out in the country and she went out there regularly once a week, returning with fruit and fresh vegetables. I think this was part of her reason for going as I had noticed that when the daughter paid a return visit they quarrelled all the time.

"You're mad," I said. "There's a doctor living just below. He'll know you're mad. I'll go to him."

"I'm not mad. The doctor's out," he said calmly. "What's more, you know the doctor is out. You said good evening to him on your way in."

"You were watching? You saw?"

"Of course. From across the road." There was a little cafe over the way, we all used it. "I chose my time."

"You didn't want to surprise your dear wife at an awkward moment?"

"I know you live here alone. You haven't remarried." I caught my breath. "I watched you come in. I knew what time to expect you."

"I don't understand all this."

"I want to stay. You understand that." He made it a statement, not a question.

"Well, you can't. We won't go into this. I don't understand you or your behaviour. I accept you're not mad. You're not normal, though. But we won't argue." I was quite cold and calm. "We'll just draw a curtain over it all, shall we? You go now and I won't say any more."

He didn't laugh, there wasn't much to laugh at for either of us. But he did smile.

"It's not as easy as that," was all he said. He moved his bag from the chair and sat down. He turned his face towards the window so that the light fell on it. He had a thin, lined face, the sort of face my husband would have had probably if he had lived until now and gone through the illness this man said he had gone through. I stared, fascinated. "You can't deny me. Don't turn me out."

I still stared; he was both strange and yet familiar. Could ten years do this to you? Ten years and a grave, I reminded myself. I looked at the bag, seeking help. No, I couldn't identify it, it was just a bag. Not ten years old, though.

You may say: "Surely you know your dead husband's face?"

But suppose your father or your brother whom you had thought dead these ten years turned up? Are you sure you would know him? People are sometimes surprisingly different from your memories. It's an idea to consider.

After my husband went, I had an illness. They called it a virus fever but it was more a sort of frenzy. I was not myself. I can remember my mother saying that, when she felt mildly unwell. It was more than that with me. I literally turned into another person. One with a high fever who raged and tore at herself and had bad dreams. The doctors put it that I reacted badly to the drugs they gave me to quell the infection.

When I came round I was ironed out as a person. It seemed to me I didn't exist. I could not think about the future and could hardly remember the past. It took me a long while to put myself together again. And I think I never wholly succeeded. My husband was one of the casualties; I suppose my mind deliberately crowded him out. I had to set to and recreate him again if I wanted to have anything to remember and it seemed to me I never did. Something was left out and I could never remember him wholly as he really had been. It was like having a bad photograph in my mind.

"It's a new bag," he said, watching my eyes. "Fairly new anyway."

The cat leapt back to its seat among the geraniums and stared down at the street below. His tail lashed back and forward.

My visitor at once got up and alertly moved to the window. He parted the geraniums and looked through. He kept half an eye on me. But he was right to move. I too had become aware of unusual noises from the street. Ours is a quiet street. I know all the noises. These were wrong.

Someone's voice was too high, too shrill. And a car was turning into the road too fast.

Down in the street one of our old city ambulances was stopping outside the cafe opposite. It is run by a Yugoslav and his wife. We can none of us think why he stays in this cold grey country instead of going to his own warm one where we all long to go on holidays. I couldn't see who it was they carried out on the stretcher. There was a grey blanket and a pair of shoes protruding from the end. It looked a burly figure. If it had been a man (and they looked like men's shoes) then he was a big one. Black-haired, too. I could just see the top of his head as they pushed him into the ambulance.

"You were over there," I said accusingly. We had been standing side by side as if we knew each other. I looked full into his face. I thought I could detect the faint remains of surprise (not shock, he was not a man who could be shocked) and yes, sadness. He had dark lines round his eyes.

He shook his head in denial.

"What about him then?" I nodded my head at the departing ambulance. "What's the matter with him?"

"A victim of the plague," he said without mirth.

"Is he dead?"

"I don't know. He looked it."

"The hospital's only just around the corner."

"Well, then, he may live." He picked up the cat, quite gently, and drew down the window. "We must talk."

I knew I should have to threaten him. I had no gun. All women living alone should have a gun. I know that now.

I had a knife, though. A long sharp steak knife, a present from Xandra. She had given it me with the joke that with cooking like mine I would always need a sharp knife. I started to move quietly towards the kitchen. The knife was out on a table near the sink. All I had to do was to get my hands on it.

I should have to get right close up to him to threaten him with a knife and I had a sick reluctance to do this. I had the terrifying idea that the closer I got the better would be my chance of recognising if he was my husband.

"I'm going to count three quietly to myself," I said, "and then I'm going to scream and scream until someone comes."

"I shouldn't."

"I made up my mind to do that if anyone broke in here when I read about the Boston Strangler." I was still moving towards the kitchen door.

"Oh, so you've heard about him," he said absently.

"Yes. Even here."

"Don't scream yet," he said, deftly producing some papers from his pocket and throwing them across to me. "I have a passport to prove who I am."

The passport certainly looked like the one my husband had taken away ten years ago, but it couldn't be because it was up to date. There was something horribly convincing about that passport. A fraud who had somehow come by my husband's passport would have had an old passport. But a man who was genuinely alive and travelling home would need a current passport; he couldn't travel on out-of-date documents. But my husband was dead, so how could he renew his passport?

"It doesn't prove anything," I said. "I can use my own eyes. I don't know who you are. But I do know who you aren't."

There were voices on the stairs. Some place down on the staircase people were talking in loud, animated, excited voices. New noises in our quiet house.

I had only to scream for help now and someone would come running. I opened my mouth.

"No, don't," he said. He moved his right hand very slightly, and let me see that it now contained a gun. I could see its round open mouth. "No shouting."

"Now I know you're not my husband," I cried out.

"I just don't want any fuss."

Feet were running up the stairs. I live on the top floor. No one comes so far up to visit me. They were pretty heavy feet and they were hurrying. Perhaps it was Anne, or Catherine. Not Xandra, she was away on tour.

Three smart taps on the door.

Then sudden relief made me start to shake.

"The door's open," I called out hoarsely.

In came the one person in the building who was no help to me at all. I'd forgotten those boots were so heavy.

He looks about eight (except for his wise, alert eyes) but I happen to know he is past twelve. I gave him those boots for his birthday.

"Hello, George," I said.

"You knew it was me?" he said cheerfully. "You recognised the sound?"

"Yes, I heard the boots." I don't know why he'd wanted those boots, but he had. He looked like a miner coming home from the pit. Once he confided in me that he thought his father had been a miner. But he didn't really know, no one knew; he was a child without a home, without a background, just a little bit of rubbish washed up by the disorganised conditions of our times. Often he looked like a gypsy; I thought he probably did have some gypsy blood in him. It would have explained a lot. At the moment he was living with a couple across the road. They loved him; I don't know if he loved them, he was sometimes untouchable. But we were friends.

"No, not my boots," he said with a frown. "My knock. Our secret knock."

"Of course." He was always creating little secrets. Such terrible things had happened to him that I think he needed the comfort of a fantasy. He was building himself a new world. Whatever happened to me, I couldn't bring fresh violence into it. "I remember the knock." I couldn't send him to get the police either. He was often in trouble with the police. Nothing serious, they just seemed to get across each other.

Out of the corner of my eye I saw that my invader had tucked himself neatly away in a corner of my top floor room where I could see him but George standing at the door could not. He still had his gun.

"Did you see the dead man across the road?" George was saying in an excited way. "The ambulance came and took him."

"He was dead?"

He nodded his head excitedly. "I was there. I was getting an ice cream. And he just seemed to drop down dead. He just curled up all neat on the table." His eyes looked big. But it wasn't the first time he'd seen death. "Best I've ever seen," he ended.

"Oh, George."

"Well, he didn't look ill or even miserable, like people usually do. He had a sort of smile and then he looked surprised. I suppose that was when . . ."

"Who was he?"

"Oh, I didn't know him." This meant he certainly wasn't a local. George knew almost everyone. "No one knew him."

He looked at me alertly. "Why are you standing there just like that? You look strange."

"I was just getting my supper."

"Yes. I can smell it. It's burning a bit." He was too clever not to sense something wrong. I wasn't so relaxed and cheerful as I usually was with him. And I hadn't immediately rushed off to rescue my supper either. "You on your own?"

"Yes."

"I thought I heard you talking."

I didn't answer. I couldn't think of the right lie. He was far too sharp to fool easily. Even as I stood there, feeling helpless, I saw his eyes fall on my intruder's little case. He didn't say anything.

"I've got to go now," he said, giving me his radiant smile. "I just wanted to come and tell you. Going to be doing any more building?"

"There's still some more work to be done to the bathroom." I was enlarging my tiny bathroom out on to the roof. It wasn't as difficult as it looked and I was doing most of it myself. George was helping.

"Don't forget when it's finished we're going to have a grand opening," he said.

"You can have first shower," I promised. It would be a mistake to think that just because he hadn't mentioned the case he wasn't thinking about it. He had his own code of good manners. But God knows what he thought.

"Goodbye," he said, as he went.

"Who's the boy?" said my invader, moving out of his corner.

"He lives round the corner."

"Not in the building?"

"No."

He nodded his head as if satisfied. He shouldn't have been. I knew George. He'd be thinking over the problem of the bag. By the time he got to the bottom of the stairs he'd have come to some conclusion.

The gun was gone. I could see my visitor wasn't the man to use its threat unless he had to.

"I'd like some coffee," I said. He followed me into the kitchen. I suppose he too was still unsteady in the momentary release from tension. George was gone. He must have thought that crisis was over; he was in and meant to stay. At all events he came up close behind me.

I picked up the knife. I meant to stick it into him as far as it would go. I knew it was murder. I felt murderous. I had my arm raised when he gripped me by the wrist. He got his thumb between the artery and the bone and dug it right in. I screamed.

The interrogator, who had a pleasant voice, said: "I hope we haven't overdone it with her and driven her mad?"

The younger one shrugged. "We had to manipulate her a little, yes. But all the reports were that she was sturdy stock; someone had to work on her before we started or we should have got nowhere. We planted one or two ideas about her husband: letter from a friend, a bill, that sort of thing. I had a telephone call planned but events moved too fast."

"And who thought of the idea of using her husband?"

"It arrived spontaneously."

"That's always dangerous, don't you think?" said the other smoothly. (He, the pleasant-voiced one, was older, and sensible.)

CHAPTER TWO

He stood there swearing at me. Not in a soft way under his breath, but in hard clipped words. He hadn't retreated, as I suppose I must have expected he would, but stood there, bolt upright, letting out a steady stream of anger at me.

"You fool. What good would it do you to have me dead in your apartment? Don't stand there. The blood is running on your sleeve."

I looked down. "The knife must have cut me."

"Serve you right."

"You might have broken my wrist." I rubbed it.

"No. Unlike you, I know when to stop."

I began to tremble. The movement started in the middle of the body as if the pelvis itself was contracting and then spread outward to the extremities.

"The trouble with you is that you don't think ahead enough," he said irritably.

"You look white yourself." He did and so did I. A brief glance in the mirror as I rushed for a towel showed me that. I looked worse than he did. "I'll get some brandy."

"Not brandy." He was irritable, but practical. "Some of that coffee. And have some yourself."

"Very dramatic," I said bitterly. "You walking in like this on me."

"Yes. It *is* dramatic." He was calm.

"I hate to say this—it gets you nowhere."

"It doesn't matter."

"If you were real, now. But you're not real. Not even a ghost. No, you're certainly not a ghost."

"No, I'm not a ghost."

"That was your only chance of having any sort of reality. I think I could have believed in you as my husband's ghost. But you're not that. So what are you then?"

"I'm on your side, at all events."

"Now that's just what I don't believe. But it's interesting to hear you talk about sides. I always suspected there were going to be sides. And who's the war between?"

"Who's it ever between?"

"Them and Us."

"That's right," he said. He said it quietly, a bit breathlessly.

The relationship between us had swung round very slightly. He was no longer the aggressor. I was now the one who had attacked him. I was no longer angry, but I was increasingly frightened of what lay ahead of me.

Then suddenly he was lying there with his eyes closed, face grey and his breathing very quick.

I rushed forward and stared into his face.

"Sorry," he said, "I don't feel so good." He closed his eyes again. His hand lay across his chest. I wondered how he had got that bracelet of scars across the wrist. Hardly knowing what I did, I picked up his other hand. Yes, scars were there too, jagged and red in the pale flesh.

"Is it your heart? I thought people like you never had hearts," I said. At least he ought to have been physically fit, I thought bitterly. "I don't want you to die a natural death."

"No," he muttered. "Just cold. Tablets in pocket." He fumbled for his pocket. I reached in and got out what he wanted. The tablets were in a small brown bottle. No name.

"Cold," he said again.

I went to the kitchen and boiled a kettle for my two hot water bottles. They were gay luxurious bottles brought back from Berlin by Xandra. She was going to spend a night with me after that trip and wanted to be sure she'd be warm.

I put the bottles round him and another blanket over the lot. And then I sat there and waited. I didn't want him to die. I was quite sure of that now. I wanted him to get up and walk out.

Gradually, as I sat there the colour came back into his face and his breathing steadied. I felt his pulse. It seemed stronger, but I was so unskilled I could not be sure.

I had a lamp turned on and the room looked comfortably and deceptively peaceful. His eyes opened once or twice and stared at me, but without expression as if he did not see me. This was alarming and I sat watching anxiously.

If he did die then I would have to decide what I was going to say. "He said he was my husband," I would begin, and they would look at me sceptically. "He wouldn't go away, I was frightened," I would say.

"Why didn't you call out, try to get help?" someone would ask.

"I was frightened."

"But why did you try to kill him?"

"I was frightened. And I didn't really mean to kill him."

"Are you sure you didn't mean to kill him?"

Was I sure I hadn't meant to kill him? What was I sure of?

"Are you so terrified of having a husband," they might ask, "that as soon as someone claims to be your husband you have to kill him?"

Perhaps that was my trouble. I hoped they wouldn't ask me that question.

Then there was the boy, George.

"Why did you tell the boy there was no one with you?" would be the next question.

"I didn't want to involve the boy in anything violent."

"Oh, so, you already knew there was going to be

violence?" I could hear that question ringing round the room. And I suppose the answer was yes, I had felt very violently towards this man from the moment he stepped through my door.

But then I realised that the sort of questions I would be asked and the way my answers were received would depend on who he was.

Who was he?

I looked towards his bag on the floor. It was a cheap plastic bag pretending to be leather. Any simple person might have carried it. I thought my intruder was more sophisticated than his bag. That is, at first glance his quiet, rather humble appearance matched his bag, but when you studied him, as I had done, you saw that he wasn't humble at all and probably not quiet. He was far more intelligent than his bag led one to believe.

I pulled the zip. I don't know what I expected to find there, a bomb perhaps, but there wasn't much. A shirt, a dressing gown, a pair of pyjamas and another pair of shoes. There was a little plastic bag of the sort that obviously contains toilet articles.

I pulled out all the clothes. Nothing was hidden in them. I ran my hand round the lining of the bag: nothing. I opened the toilet bag. Only an old fashioned razor and some soap. He meant to stay then. He had packed his bag for a visit.

Nothing in the bag was quite new, but nothing was much used either. The razor was the only old object. I picked it up and examined it. Heavy English work and much used. If he was as old as his razor he was older than he looked. I tried to think what sort of razor my husband had used, but I couldn't remember. I hadn't been interested. It could have been one like this, though.

I looked at the still face. You'd think you'd be able to look at a face and say "That's not the face of the man I married", but I couldn't. This was an older face, a changed face, it wasn't the same face, but ten years is a long time. I remembered my mother seeing herself in a mirror once before she died and saying "That poor old thing looks ill," without knowing it was herself.

I repacked the bag, not with particular care. I didn't mind if he knew. But there was nothing in his bag to give him a name.

He was a nameless man.

And a nameless man is something dangerous to get involved with in our society.

I looked again at his face. Potentially it was a tragic face.

Moved by an unexplained curiosity I went over to the mirror to look at my own face, to see if tragedy was there too.

As I watched I realised that he was sleeping. He had drifted into a light sleep. I knew it was light, because he stirred at my every movement. I thought once or twice he was on the point of saying something.

I sat there waiting. After about fifteen minutes, he suddenly opened his eyes wide, sat up and swung into a sitting position.

"I needed that sleep," he said.

"And the tablets," I said.

"I won't die of it, you know."

"I'd guessed."

"And I wouldn't have dropped off now if I hadn't been a little short of sleep. I know what to do for myself."

I was silent. I thought in fact he was disconcerted that he had fallen asleep, that, even unwell, he had expected alertness from himself. Not for the first time it struck me that he was no stranger to physical violence, had formed some idea how he would behave under it. Apparently this time he hadn't run true to form.

"Are you a doctor, then?"

"You know I'm not a doctor. I have some quack medicine."

"All right then, charlatan," I said. "Get up and walk."

He looked up in surprise. "I'm asking you for help."

"And I'm telling you to go."

He leaned back against the sofa. "You can attack me again if you like. If you think you're up to it. Otherwise, I accept your invitation to stay."

"You don't harrow me," I said. All the same I knew I should not attack him again. Not yet.

I walked out of the room and went to get some water and another clean towel.

He was lying back on the sofa with his feet up again. He looked better, but not well.

"You can't get rid of me now," he said; he gave a slight smile.

I was beginning to see that I couldn't.

"It's comfortable here," he said, looking round.

"Not changed since you knew it last?" I enquired sceptically.

He refused the gambit. "Memories change in ten years," he said. "You forget. What you remember isn't there and you suddenly realise it never was. Memories are very treacherous."

It was a clever answer really, because of course this apartment had changed greatly since I had lived here alone. I hadn't done it on purpose, but it had happened naturally and imperceptibly over the years. I had painted the walls and moved the furniture, broken some things and altered others, replaced a carpet and recovered a chair. There was nothing very new in the apartment, but everything in it now reflected me.

"*I* can remember what it was like ten years ago," I said.

"Can you?" He looked amused. "But then you've gone on living here."

"Lucky me," I said bitterly. I hadn't realised before the bitterness was in me. People said how well I'd adjusted to losing a husband, how mature and well balanced I was, making my own career and being such a good mother to Justine. I'd believed them. Now I knew that all the time I had been bitterly, furiously angry at being widowed. In my heart I had decided that my husband's death had been so unnecessary. No one had made him go off to the dig where he had been killed; he had chosen to go. Eagerly he had embarked on a course which could only lead to his death. I resented this.

It was quite a shock to find out how I felt. All these years beneath my sorrow and my braveness I had been cherishing this hard little nugget. No wonder I hadn't remarried. I wasn't looking for happiness any more but revenge.

It looked as though I had the chance to take it now. That hand that had picked up the knife hadn't been ill advised. Here was a man who claimed he was my husband: let him bear his punishment.

"Yes," I said. "I've gone on living here. I've gone on living and growing. I suppose I've changed too. Do you think I've changed?" He ought to think I had.

"Physically not very much."

"And mentally? Emotionally?"

"I'm beginning to think you have."

"You're right. I have." I got up. "Well, you might as well stay the night, anyway. You can sleep on that sofa. We can talk in the morning." I spoke pleasantly.

I got him another blanket and a pillow. I was tired and hungry, but I felt no desire to eat the supper still in my oven. I didn't care how hungry he was. And I thought he *was* hungry probably, and over-spent all round. More and more he looked to me like a man who knew tension.

"Tell me," I said, just before I left. "How have I changed?"

"You're curious to see what I say?"

"Of course."

He studied me, thinking. It must have been quite a problem. My appearance he could have learned from photographs but my character would be more difficult to ascertain.

He considered. "You've built up a side of yourself that didn't exist those years ago. You're more creative. That's your work, I suppose. That didn't exist then."

"It was beginning." But what he said meant nothing. Plenty of people knew about my work. I was even beginning to be well known.

"But at the same time you're less decisive. I think you may be slower to make up your mind."

"I've had more decisions to take. Sometimes that makes you more hesitant not less." But he was holding his own well and making some good guesses. If I had changed at all then this was the way in which I had changed.

"You know about the career I've made?"

"Oh yes, I was reading about it on the way home." He had a curiously honest way of putting it. In some way or another this was exactly what he had done. I don't know what counted as home, though. "In a magazine." I knew the article. I didn't get into magazines very often. This month was the first time. Handy for him. It had given some personal details about me. Knowing he had read this article explained quite a lot.

"That was an old photograph of me," I said, not without irony.

"Yes. A bad one. You're prettier," he answered gravely.

"You don't remember that photograph?"

"No. Should I?"

"You took it."

"Don't try and catch me that way. The photograph was an old one, yes. But not that old. Women weren't wearing their hair like that ten years ago. Nor a dress like that. Say five at the most."

It had been taken four years ago. Perhaps we're a bit slow about fashion. He'd been an acute observer of life in that prison or grave of his.

I started to go again. "Wait a minute," he said, putting out a hand. "Just now you had a burst of thoughts that checked you. They were thoughts about your own nature."

"What a lot you know about my mind."

"I know a lot about imprisonment," he said. "You are in a prison now."

He was quiet for a moment, then started again.

"But I want you to know that these are natural and inevitable thoughts in your circumstances. It is how the human mind reacts; you are not to blame yourself. And soon they will go."

He had read my thoughts and now he was being sympathetic. I was furious.

"There's one person you've forgotten who's going to take an interest in you and your return," I said from the door.

"Who's that?"

"Teddy. Don't tell me you've forgotten Teddy."

In the night I woke myself with tears. Tears and tears. What was I crying for?

"Your father's back," I said to Justine on the telephone next morning. My guest was still asleep on his sofa.

"What?"

I repeated it. "Your father's back. At least, he says he's your father. I want you to come round and see."

"But he's dead." I could tell she was still sleepy and not understanding what I was saying.

"He may not be your father. I want you to come and look."

"But I won't *know*." Her voice was rising. "Is he still there?"

"Yes. Asleep."

"You let him stay? All night?"

"If he is your father, Justine, I couldn't very well turn him out. Besides . . . there were other reasons."

"Yes," said Justine in a strange voice.

"He's asleep on the *sofa*, Justine."

She gave a faint giggle and it occurred to me that I really knew nothing about Justine's life. Perhaps she did not believe in living entirely for her work. I had met some of her friends and they all seemed as hard-working and dedicated as herself.

"Dearest," said Justine, with that laugh still in her voice. "You don't change. I'll be round."

I felt strong this morning. Anger makes you strong; love makes you weak. Or is it the other way round? I knew there was a strong current of some emotion running through me, but so far it did not have a name.

"I'll be ringing Teddy, too," I promised.

"Oh, Teddy," said Justine with a groan, before she rang off.

Whether my visitor truly remembered Teddy or had never heard of him, he was not likely to feel pleasure at the introduction of his name. Teddy was the great man in our family, but no one had ever enjoyed thinking about him. Or perhaps his wife had once. He had a wife, a well dressed machine-like woman. No, remembering her, I decided she had married Teddy for the sake of her ambition. Teddy was my husband's elder brother and they were all that the war had left of a once large family. But there was no doubt that Teddy had survived and prospered. Today he had a large rather ugly flat overlooking the river, a big car and his machine-like wife with her fur coat.

Teddy had to be informed. I lifted up the telephone and tried to get through. No answer. They must be away. They had a little house in the country and went down there as often as they could.

I wasn't sorry. Teddy was going to take some talking to. I could just hear him, using his precise, official voice.

"What's this about my brother? My dear girl, are you out of your mind? We investigated the matter thoroughly at the time, you know. I showed you the report. Done by a very good man. Impeccable bit of work. No, no, there's no question about it, your husband is dead. He won't come back."

Yes, Teddy would think I was mad, but he had to be told. There was this about Teddy's position, you felt you had to tell him things. Poor Teddy, I suppose he had *some* friends. A few lowly souls who didn't mind looking upwards at him and were grateful for the patronage he could bestow. For Teddy had power —not the best sort of power, the sort that is open, manifest and breeds generosity—but the small secret sort that creates only a mystique.

Our mystique about Teddy was that whatever favours you got from him did you no good in the end.

It was Saturday. I didn't have to go to work. It was going to be a quiet weekend and I could stay home and attend to my problem.

I put the coffee pot on the tray and went into the sitting room. I don't know what I expected, really, on the other side of the door. Perhaps I hoped he had gone.

I gathered up my courage and walked in.

My invader had the sofa tidied and was sitting in a chair by the window looking out when I walked in. You couldn't see much from a chair, except roof tops; you had to stand up and put your head over the geraniums to see the street.

He turned and looked at me sombrely as I came in. He got up. He was moving a bit stiffly. Well, that was my fault.

I put the tray on the round table without speaking. Normally, when I was alone I had breakfast here where I could drink my coffee with the sun warming me. If this seems too leisured and luxurious let me add I only sat down at the weekends, the rest of the week I stood.

I poured him some coffee and took it over.

"You're late," he said, thus showing once again how well he knew my habits. "You were telephoning?"

I didn't answer. Of course he had listened. He would have been a fool if he hadn't.

"So Justine is coming round." He drank some coffee.

He must be guessing? He couldn't possibly have heard anything of Justine's side of the conversation.

"Good," he said.

"You're pleased?"

"Of course." He finished his coffee. "We shall see what she makes of me."

"Aren't you afraid she'll take one look at you and say: 'I've never seen you before in my life'?"

"I'll be surprised if she does that." Without asking, he came over and poured himself some more coffee, took some bread and butter. The bread was close textured and a little stale but he ate it with pleasure.

"How is your wound?"

"It is stiff, sore, but not, I think, infected," I told him.

"You should be glad. It means we will not have to call in a doctor, which is better for me, and," he added pleasantly, "also for you."

I couldn't mistake the threat, politely but clearly delivered. I hardly ever saw my doctor. He seemed a kind man but I couldn't say how he'd react to the story of a stabbing, and whose version of events he would believe. I don't think he wanted to be involved in any trouble any more than anyone else. No one did these days. These days were no worse than any other days, I suppose, except now there was a sort of hope in people's hearts that if you hung on you might emerge into a happier world. And no one wanted to risk that hope.

"I'd like to know what a doctor would make of you," I said thoughtfully. "He might be able to tell me something I'd like to know. Things I ought to know, come to that."

"Such as?"

"Such as where you have been for the last ten years and what your physical state has been."

"Whether I am mad or not, you mean?"

"Physical," I said, "not mental. What you've been doing, the sort of life you've led. I'd rather not know about your mind. A man who can come in here and say he is my husband . . ." I shrugged.

He looked at me rather sadly and then drank some more coffee. "You're hard," he said. "Harder than I expected."

"I could ask Justine for a diagnosis," I said. "She's a scientist."

"Not a doctor, though."

"No. She says herself she works in the area where biochemistry and biology touch. Something to do with mutations. But she might have an idea or two about you." I looked at him appraisingly. "I would say you could be a diabetic. That could be brought on by shock or strain, and you've had those, I'd say."

My door bell rang very loudly.

"Justine," said my visitor, not moving.

"No, not Justine, she doesn't ring the door bell like that."

I'd forgotten it was Saturday. My friend Elizabeth, wife of the owner of the café across the way, stood there.

"Brought your bread over," she said. On Saturday and Sunday she brought me over a batch of her own baking. She made lovely bread. She was small and round, rather the shape of one of her own crusty loaves, and she made me think of a nursery world with fields of bright tall sunflowers and storks flying over them. "Did you hear about yesterday evening? It was awful."

"I saw the ambulance from the window."

"You didn't see the police afterwards? That poor man! He looked so respectable but I think he must have been in trouble the way the police were round asking questions. Of course, we'd never seen him before in our lives." She sounded relieved.

"Do you think he killed himself?"

"Oh, I don't see how he could have. He was sitting there drinking his coffee and suddenly he dropped down. I never saw anything like it."

"That's what George said."

"That boy." She sounded irritated. "He'd no business being there, seeing things like that." She put her parcel of bread down on the table and noticed the extra cup. My visitor had made himself scarce. He knew all the tricks. "Had Justine with you?" she asked.

"Yes," I said with a smile. I don't know whether she believed me or not. She knew Justine's habits as well as mine and it was three years since Justine spent the night here.

"What a night we've had. I couldn't sleep a wink. It upsets you, that sort of thing. Your light was on late, too."

"Was it?" I was surprised. Time hadn't meant anything last night.

"You don't look as if you had too good a night yourself." She was studying my face. "And then today the police round again before breakfast. Looking round everywhere, showing us photographs. Did we know him? Had we seen him before?" She gathered herself up to go. "Mark my words, that was no ordinary death and he was no ordinary man."

"No."

"Anyway, the other thing I came to say was that the police are going round everywhere asking questions and showing this photograph. They'll be calling on you." Her eyes rested on that cup and saucer, and then I knew she hadn't believed me.

"I'd better get dressed then."

"Yes, I should do that. Oh, don't worry. The one I had was a nice young man. You know him—the one who lives round the corner by the taxi rank. His wife had a baby last week. No, he's all right. It's the one with him I don't like."

"There's two of them then?"

"Oh, they always go round in pairs. You know that."

I knew.

"Well, the second one of this pair's got nasty black eyes, a bruise on his nose and a grouse on his shoulders. You'll have to watch him. He's going to break someone's life if he can."

"It's like that?"

"Oh, nothing personal; he'll do it from the best possible motives and get promotion from it too."

I picked up her bread, preparatory to taking it through to the kitchen. "I shan't worry too much," I said casually. "After all, it's nothing to do with me."

"Are you sure?"

I stopped dead. I had moved about half a foot nearer my kitchen. From my new position I could see my visitor sitting calmly on a chair by the cooker. He gave the impression however of listening to our conversation. "No, I never knew the man. How could it be anything to do with me?"

"It's just an impression I got." She seemed undecided whether to go on or keep quiet. "I could be wrong, but I've got used to watching people and weighing them up. I just wonder what he was doing there."

"He was sitting there having a cup of coffee and getting ready to die."

"If he was doing anything he was watching."

She took a deep breath.

"If he was watching anyone, it was you. He saw you come in."

"Now you're frightening me."

"The police may know that, may know he was watching you. They'll want to ask questions."

I stood there clutching the bread; it was hard and cold and not fresh baked at all. "How can they know he was watching me?"

"They have their ways. Then again, he might have been a policeman. That struck me as soon as I saw him."

She had been very good to come and tell me all this. The bread was just an excuse. She was not one of those who would keep out of someone else's trouble.

"Thanks for telling me," I said hoarsely.

When she'd gone, I walked over to the kitchen and banged on the door.

"You heard all that?" I asked. "Don't pretend it has nothing to do with you."

"I don't pretend it has nothing to do with me," he said, walking out of the kitchen.

"Was he a policeman?"

"I hope not," he said.

"When the policemen come I shall tell them about you. How you came, all you've done. If you're still here, that is."

"I shall still be here. You'll have to hide me. I'm afraid I'm with you for a long time yet."

"If I tell the police they'll take you away."

"Oh yes, no doubt. But they'll take you too." I looked at him quickly. "There are so many things you don't know. To be on the safe side the police will take you too. Think you can stand it?"

"I should soon be home again." But my voice was thick.

"Don't be so sure. And then there's Justine. What about her? Don't think she's going to escape. She's already on her way round now, isn't she?"

He was hinting at a nightmare. I was in it, Justine was in it, and he, this strange man who wished me to call him husband was in it.

"I'm here to stay," he said softly. "Better get used to it."

When the policemen came I was dressed and working at my desk. The two of them came together as predicted, the young kind one and the middle-aged one with black harsh eyes. They were very polite to me and I was very polite back. We hadn't come to a stage in our relationship where anything but politeness was demanded of us. With luck we never would.

They showed me a photograph. I didn't know this face, I said. And no, I didn't think he knew me, but of this one couldn't of course be quite sure. I smiled and nodded slightly, they smiled and nodded slightly. What did he die of? I asked, but they didn't answer. Perhaps it was the plague. That was quite an answer. Maybe we had the first case of the plague here in the city, had the Black Death with us.

"That must be the answer," I said to my visitor, as he emerged from his hiding place in the back of my kitchen cupboard. I'll tell you about that cupboard. It's so huge I am thinking of building it out into another little room when I have finished with the bathroom. It should jut out on to the roof and be no trouble to anyone. I have the bricks all ready. "He died of the plague." I didn't mean it to come out bitterly, but it certainly did, a mean, hard sound.

"There was nothing much to that visit of theirs," he said. "They were just checking, just looking over."

"It felt as painful to me as if it was important."

He looked at me as if I was going to have to be stronger than that. I knew it too.

"I'm dressed and you're dressed," I said. "The day is fully here, isn't it time we had a talk?"

He grimaced.

"You can't still go on saying you are my husband, can you? I never believed you. For a moment I thought to myself perhaps it could be, perhaps he survived to come back to me, but I didn't deceive myself for long."

"Well, I don't know about that," he began; he was a joker.

"No, you're not what you say you are, but you are here. I have a right to know why you are here."

He had turned up on my doorstep and presented me with a problem. He had involved himself in my past

as well as my present. This could not be accident. I had
to ask myself what in my life had caused him to happen. He had called up questions about my past as well
as my future. What had I been, what had I done to
bring him to my door? After all, he wasn't the sort of
thing who happened to everyone, was he?

He moved across the room and sat down on the sofa.
"I am in some pain," he said, "not much, but a little."
So that was what the grimace had meant.

"Oh, yes?" I said, not believing much in the pain.

I had misjudged him, though, the muscles in his
hands and wrists were rigid with pain. They were
knotted right up like rope.

"You minded those policemen coming a lot more
than I did," I said.

"No, no it was cold in that cupboard."

"If the rest of you feels stiff the way your hands do,
you need something," I said. I went to the glass-
fronted cabinet under the window and got out a
bottle. This slivovitz was another present from Xandra,
from Belgrade this time.

We both drank.

"It's so big and huge and cold that cupboard of
yours. You could live in it."

"This is a cold flat. Always has been. *You* should
know that." I finished my slivovitz rapidly. I could
see you could get a taste for it. "You know plenty
about me and this place, don't you? You had the information scraped up and put together for you to use."

"All right." He held up a hand as if announcing a
decision. "We declare a moratorium on whether I am
your husband. I don't ask you to believe and you don't
ask questions."

"No?" I started to laugh. "You surprise me. I was
beginning to get hooked."

When those policemen were with me I had thought
first of all they knew I was hiding something from
them, then later on I thought no; they are genuinely
at a loss, just asking around. Then I thought if that

man who got killed was watching me they don't know it. Finally I was beginning to think that he hadn't watched me at all and that there was no one in the cupboard and it was all imagination. (And mine too, of course.) Then they showed me the photograph of the dead man.

Now I'll tell you about a funny thing. About the photograph.

It was a photograph of my husband. Or it could have been. An older, thinner face. Also, once again, a dead face. It's difficult to tell about dead faces. Especially about a face which in your mind's eye (that unpredictable organ) has been dead, then alive and now dead again.

That was why I was laughing.

Naturally he wasn't pleased at my laughing. Not having seen the photograph he didn't know what to make of it. I didn't think I'd tell him either. It was getting to be the time for him to tell me things.

Perhaps he was just going on to tell me why he was not my husband when the telephone rang. One short little burst of noise which somehow meant nothing good.

"I could ignore it." I looked at him.

"No. Answer it." He walked away to the window where the cat Atabi was sunning himself.

"Hello?"

"Stella?" It was Justine. "Stella, are you alone?"

"Not entirely," I said cautiously. But she knew what I meant.

"Just him? Not the police?"

"No." I was surprised. What could Justine know about the call from the police?

"They may come." Her voice was anxious and distressed. "It's what stopped me coming to see you. You don't know?"

"Know what?" My voice was sharp. I knew plenty of terrible things. Which one has she fixed on?

"It's Uncle Teddy. You didn't telephone him?"

"No," I said, my heart like a stone.

"He's killed himself. Teddy has killed himself." She might have been crying. She hadn't much liked Teddy, alive, but she had tears. "He shot himself this morning. He must have got up early, gone into his own workroom and shot himself."

I put the receiver down although she was still talking. "Teddy's dead," I said. "He's shot himself."

He nodded. He didn't seem surprised. It was less than twenty-four hours since he had turned up on my doorstep and already two men were dead.

CHAPTER THREE

"Teddy didn't kill himself for nothing. I know Teddy. He was a desperate clinger to life. If he killed himself it was because he was terribly afraid."

"If you cut a hole in the floor of your house then you're going to fall through it one day."

"And that's what Teddy did?"

"It's what we all do, I suppose," he said rather sadly. "We all have a hole in our floor, only his hole got bigger and bigger."

It was hard to take in that Teddy, the big success man, was no longer with us. Hard to believe that I ought to feel sorry for his highly mechanised wife.

The cat walked around the centre of the room lashing his tail; he was obviously delighted to have company in the middle of the day. Normally he lived such a lonely life.

We were desperately scrabbling for a relationship, this man and I. We had to form something or we should fall through any number of holes in the floor. The relationship he had laid claim to was one of love and trust. But everything that had happened since he came filled me with fear and suspicion.

It was all my own fault. I had let him in through the door when he came. I should have slammed it in his face. But I had been a victim to the oldest feminine weakness in the book. I had let my mind play a trick on me. "Danger," one part of me had alerted. "Yes, but he looks terribly interesting. You might like to know him," another part of my mind had accurately stated. I had let myself down and I deserved everything I was getting. And even as I said this to myself another part of me was wondering how I was going to enjoy it.

I looked at him sitting there and, I declare, I even felt sorry for him. He couldn't possibly match me in duplicity.

The cat jumped on his lap and stared in his face, a rare mark of affection. If it was affection. Sometimes I felt that the steady penetrating gaze he fixed on one showed something more menacing, and that it would not have done to be his size.

"Tell me the truth," I said.

"You're too clever a person to think I can do that easily. Or completely."

"None of your philosophy, now," I said. "None of this talk about truth being hard to know and what is truth and so on and so on. Just a set of facts, such as common ordinary minds like mine call truth. Such as why you are here, what you are doing and who you are. Especially who you are."

He smiled at me and stroked the cat's head. I could have told him that this would do him no good at all with Atabi, who immediately wrenched himself away and galloped insolently to the window. "You are clever," he said.

"The truth," I said relentlessly.

"We shall have to have some truth from you too," he said. "I haven't been too explicit with you until now. As a matter of fact, I've been waiting to see if you said anything."

"I've said plenty."

"Not what I've been expecting to hear."

I stared at him.

"Remember we know all about you."

"Everyone knows all about me," I said sourly. "I live a very open life, more's the pity. Who's we?"

"Me and my friends."

"Oh, you have some? I thought you were a man without a friend, a man on your own."

"From now on I shall have to be." He sounded grim.

No jokes now. "I came here for a specific purpose. I suppose you could call it a mission. I had reason to think you would accept me."

As, in a sense, I had.

"I don't know why you thought that."

"Yes, you have been rather reserved. I congratulate you on being able to keep your own counsel," he said.

"I don't know what you mean."

"We'll go into that later. At all events, I did not believe you would turn me from the door. Nor did you. We'd investigated you, you see."

I was beginning to see that.

"And, of course, you know what I am," he added.

"No," I cried, "no."

He stared, then shrugged. "Very well. I'll play it your way if you like. It's safer perhaps. Safer for you. Very well. You do not know who I am."

"What is your name?"

"You can call me Stephen."

But Stephen was one of my husband's names, his second, bestowed on him by his godfather. I didn't like his offer; he was still putting forward his claim to be my husband.

He smiled at me as if to say: all right, I won't rush you. You are in a strange position.

He gave a little half bow, I swear he did. "However I may seem to you, however well assimilated, I am in fact a foreigner, a stranger. It's not noticeable. I think I look at home. I'm meant to look at home. I suppose you could say I am hidden. Hidden in the community."

"Our community," I said, with significance.

"Your community." Again that little half bow. We both avoided the use of the word country. Patriots both, I suppose, in our way.

"You are a spy? An agent?"

"That makes it sound more important than I am."
All the same, I thought he was important.

"Are you a Russian?" I asked bluntly.

"No." He laughed. "Do I look like one?"

I shook my head. He did not look like a Russian. I had not thought he was one. There was mixed blood in him.

"And now," he went on, "the time has come for me to go into deeper hiding. Here. With you. I want you to hide me."

This was the moment for me to scream and run for help. To call for Justine, to summon Teddy, to close the family ranks and squeeze the intruder out.

But Teddy was dead. Teddy was already dead.

It takes some getting used to a statement like that. The whole situation took some getting used to.

"Why me?" I said at last. "What makes you think I want you here or that I'm going to let you stay?" I got up and started to move around. "I've been irresolute and very cowardly," I said, "but this has to end. You can't stay here, it's quite impossible and aren't you afraid I'll tell the police what you've just told me?"

"No, I'm not afraid of that," he said decisively. "And of course I shall stay here."

"Why? Why should I let you?"

"You have to."

We kept playing this game: you can't stay; I will stay; I won't let you stay; you have to let me stay. The threats he offered were various, first he was my husband, then he had a gun, then he held an unknown threat over my head. But now I felt we were getting near to the bone.

Teddy had killed himself and another man had died. I had to remember that. I called it a game, but it was no game.

"No. I won't do it. I know I've sometimes felt a stranger, an alien, but that's in the past now. I'm one of them now. This is my life. I belong. I have made it my own."

"If I could walk out of here and leave you to your own life, believe me I would. But you'd never get away with it."

"I'd never get away with it." My voice was rising.

"I like that way of putting it. You're the one trying for that."

Outside in the street a brass band was walking down the street. We had Saturday morning concerts in the summer in the square round the corner. They were playing a polka: the Fisherman's Polka. I used to play it myself, on the piano, as a schoolgirl.

"You're too well documented to escape," he said. "What there is to know about you we know."

"Except my temper, except my state of mind."

"Yes, I grant you that may have changed with the years. Perhaps there are things you regret, but it's too late now. You have to measure up to what's expected of you."

"I don't understand you."

"It's going to be difficult to keep that attitude up." His expression had hardened. So too, no doubt, had mine.

"I'm going to call the police. I shall tell them what you've told me."

"Yes. You can do that. They'll believe you. Be glad to."

"I have to protect myself."

"You think you are doing that?"

"Yes." I didn't want to sacrifice him, I never want to sacrifice anyone, but there wasn't only myself, there was Justine.

"Then I shall tell them that you are a sleeper," he said gently.

A sleeper. For a moment I fumbled for his meaning.

"One of us," he went on. "Someone we had planted in the population against our future use. A silent unknown partner."

"It's not true." My voice was horrible, so rough and coarse.

"Don't you remember as a student joining a certain society?" he said cruelly. "Don't you remember taking a sum of money? Don't you remember a solemn oath you swore?"

CHAPTER FOUR

Only Anne could have told him. It must have been
Anne. It must have been one of our group, and I
thought it was Anne. I couldn't be sure, just at that
moment, why the image of Anne came into my mind,
but it did. I loved Anne, this is something I must never
forget, but of all my three friends I suppose she has
given me most pain. She is the cleverest, to begin with,
and therefore her powers to hurt are stronger; and
she is beautiful, and that undoubtedly helps her. With-
drawn, living by her own standards, she isn't easy to
get to know. She has a temper, too. I know this is what
worried her husband. The last time I saw them they
had been reunited after one of their periodical separa-
tions. They were back together in Anne's beautiful old-
fashioned flat overlooking the river. From her sitting-
room window you can see the river run swirling past.
It runs fast where she lives. A man was drowned there
a few weeks ago. Come to think of it, our meeting was
at that time. The man had drowned the night I visited
her. What a lot of deaths there were about me lately.

I wondered when and how my visitor had been in
touch with Anne. I looked at him sitting there, relatively at ease.

"I was a little more political when I was a student,"
I admitted. "Perhaps I did join a society or two. I'd
like to point out I joined several."

"And at least one of those societies had a more secret
side."

"Perhaps."

"You know it had."

I pushed the memory aside. "We were only students. It was not important."

"Well, there I disagree. It's important to me and it must be important to you. It was on the secret side you took your money and were retained on our strength."

It was a monstrous thing to say, and he made no attempt to hide its monstrosity.

"I never took any money. I never made any promises."

"It is in the records. You knew we should be calling on you."

"No," I cried.

There was silence.

"Then it's your word against mine," he said.

I was suddenly and furiously angry. There I was, in the middle of a quiet, creative life, and he walked in. He had shattered my composure and managed to hang on to his own. I thought that he even seemed faintly pleased with himself. He looked at me calmly, apparently not noticing my anger: he didn't know me well enough yet to know my anger was dangerous. Or perhaps I was wrong there; he had had one taste of it.

I began to think about what I could do. I felt the first thing was to make him keep quiet. His words had so much power. I felt his strength all the time. He was making me believe things I didn't want to believe. About the money, for instance, and promises I might have made.

He gave me that sort of half bow again, goodness knows where he had learnt to behave like that, and that decided me.

"All right then," I said. "I'll go along with you. I'll tell you what you want to know."

"Good."

I put my hand on my throat. "I must get a drink first, I feel strangely thirsty."

He nodded. "It's strain." He half rose to his feet.

"No. I'll go." I pushed him back in his chair. "Just water. I'll get a drink in the kitchen."

I turned to the kitchen. As I went I let my hand
trail lightly down his shoulder. He looked faintly
surprised; I will say that for him. I smiled at him.

I went out to the kitchen and I did take a drink; I
was thirsty and he was quite right, it *was* nerves. But
after a long cold drink I went to my big cupboard.
You need all sorts of things when you are bricklaying
and it also gives you good strong muscles in the arms.
I plucked out what I needed, put it into my pocket,
and went back into the room.

He was sitting there with his head leaning against
the back of the chair. He looked tired. I came up behind him; he did not stir. I put my hands gently over
his eyes. Then I brushed his face as I let my hands drop
to his shoulders. I rested my hands on them. He stayed
quite still. I let my hands gently stroke down his arms.
I thought I felt a slight reaction in his muscles. I
smiled. I could see his face reflected in the mirror on
the wall; it was quite impassive. He could see my face
too; he was watching me. Then he closed his eyes.

Still smiling, I drew from my pocket the length of
thin rope that I had secreted there. It's extraordinary
the odd things you need when you're doing any sort
of building.

Still keeping my eyes on his face, still smiling, I
drew the cord round his shoulders. He reacted at once,
but I had drawn it tight just above his elbows, tether-
ing him to the back of the chair before he could stop
me.

He tried to wrench himself free, kicking his feet out.
But that chair was top heavy, as I well knew, and he
fell backwards. I think he must have given his head a
blow against the wall as he went down. Anyway, he
was still for a bit, and I seized this moment to start
tying his ankles to the legs of the chair.

He threshed around trying to struggle but he didn't
have much chance, the initiative was with me and I
was determined. All in all, I thought he put up a weak
fight. Even so, we were both panting by the time I had

him tied and the chair the right way up. I had considered leaving him lying on his back, but I like things
neat.

"I wonder what the people underneath made of that
noise?" I said aloud. I had my hand over his mouth.

We were still panting and glaring at each other when
the door bell rang.

"Well, we'll soon see," I said.

The questioner said: "What really happened there?
There seems to me absolutely no reason to believe a
word she says."

"Oh yes. You can believe her. Sort of," said the
other, younger man wearing a brown suit. "I'm afraid
we overdid her manipulation. Whether she understood
it or not she was being profoundly influenced. Let me
put it like this: all the things she says are true, but she
sees them a little distorted. Her emotions are height-
ened. As in a nightmare."

"A planned nightmare."

"Oh, of course, she was in a susceptible state to begin
with. Due to fall."

"Down into hate?"

The younger man laughed. His brown suit was a
little tight for him as if he had got fatter or the suit
had shrunk from over much cleaning. Prosperity was
not for him this year. Next year, perhaps. He had a
scar down one side of his face. It was not a new scar,
but had faded over two or three years.

Before going to the door I turned back and tied his
mouth up with his own large white handkerchief. His
hands were already tethered. I waved as I went. "Ta,
ta," I said. I was consumed with a terrible sort of insolent coquetry. I had never experienced it before, but
I had absolutely no trouble in recognising it for what
it was.

Antoinette, my friend the hairdresser from the floor

below, was outside. She was back from her night in the the country.

"Whatever was that terrible noise?" she said. "Are you all right?"

She is a square woman with a coiffure of round bubble curls like a little girl, but her face is mature.

"Just my bricks fell down."

"You builders!" She spread out her hands. "Thought you'd killed yourself. You will one day. You'll lie up there dead and none of us will know."

"It's an idea," I said. In various shapes and forms it had already occurred to me. It would be easy enough for me to die; it might come to that yet.

"Well, I'll pop down again. I'm making some soup. Fresh vegetable soup. Not that the carrots are so good. I've blunted my knife cutting these carrots, you can't get decent vegetables," she grumbled. "It'll be good soup, though."

"I can smell it." She always made a great supply of soup every Saturday and lived on it all the week. Or so I thought. She stumped off down the stairs and I waved to her. In my book, she was a friend, in spite of that smell of onions and beans and lentils she created every Saturday.

Back in my room, I looked again at my capture. Necessarily his expression was not easy to read.

"Don't worry," I said, going up and speaking to his eyes, "I'm not going to do anything. I just want a lull. You can understand that, can't you? A rest, really. You're a bit too much for me."

I took a cigarette from a box on the table and sat down to smoke it.

"I shall have to think what to do, though," I said. "You've given me a problem. Yes, quite a problem." I smiled at him brilliantly. At least, I hoped it was brilliant. Certainly it must have had a good cutting edge on it.

The telephone rang. It was Justine. She sounded nervous, edgy.

Straight away she said, "Can you come out and meet me?"

"Yes, I think so." I did think so.

"What about . . ." she hesitated, "your visitor?"

I looked at him. He was sitting there thinking things over. I wished I'd remembered to remove his gun before I tied him up. I gave him a wintry smile. "He's not giving me much trouble," I said.

"In the gardens then, by the river. I'm going to walk there." The gardens were one of Justine's playgrounds as a girl. We had paced round and round them in silence in the weeks when her father was first missing. There was a boy who used to meet her there, too. In the days of agony when her father was lost he used to stand in the gardens and watch us walk together. I wondered where he was now.

"I'll be there," I said. To my visitor, I said: "I'm going out for a short while." I checked his bonds. "You ought to be quite safe." I looked around. "But just to make quite sure I'll pop you into my nice big kitchen cupboard where no one can see you."

There was a long scrape on the kitchen linoleum where I dragged his chair backwards through the kitchen. He was heavy but you can get a good purchase on a chair if you tilt it. I did it in stages, having a rest every so often. Even so my arms ached when I'd finished.

I closed and double-locked the door behind me and ran down the stairs. In the street outside it was warm and sweet. I bent my head back to look upward and could just see my geraniums and Atabi among them.

I did not cross the bridge but crossed the tram lines and walked eastward along the river embankment with the sun shining in my face. Very soon I passed the apartment block with the statues on the roof and the great curving iron balconies. Art Nouveau, built about 1900. Anne lived there, at the moment with her husband, sometimes without.

I looked up at her windows, I remembered our last

meeting. Anne was strange that evening. She did not kiss me when we met, and maintained a formal manner. She could do that. It only meant that for some reason, probably nothing to do with me, she was not at her ease. Perhaps Anne had played the informer on me. It could be. She and I had been very close at one time.

Soon I passed the old rococo church where so many visitors called to see the wax image of the Holy Innocent in all his fine jewels. This wasn't the famous Holy Innocent, of course, but our local doll. There was an old woman going up the steps now behind an American tourist. She'd wait until the American came out again, and then offer her postcards of the doll. Rather poor ones, too. I used to be very fond of that old church before they spoilt it. All over the city scaffolding is going up as repairs are made to buildings left grubby and neglected for years. I suppose it's a sign of prosperity, but in some ways I liked the dirt. At least it stopped us looking like Chicago.

The sun was out, the river sparkled and I found that I was enjoying the sight. I was almost happy. Do you know that feeling when, in spite of everything that oppresses your mind, your body goes on holiday? It must pass, this minute, but for the moment I enjoyed it.

It did pass. I saw Justine, head down, hands in pockets, pacing the garden, and in a moment was as unhappy as you could wish.

"My dear," I said.

She took my hand; her own was cold. Underneath her summer tan she was very white. Still, she was as carefully dressed as ever. Lately, her appearance had worried me. She was adopting a sort of austerity, with her hair cut short and her hands scrubbed with short nails. I wondered sometimes if this was connected with her work.

"Justine, are you in trouble?"

"Not me, no."

But there was that look about her of trouble that was both immediate and personal. Yet her words belied it.

"No, it's not me. Not me more than anyone. It's us. All of us. Us as a family," she said, looking straight at me. "That's why I wanted to talk to you here. Outside."

"So everybody could see us?"

"No. So they couldn't. So all the people in Teddy's flat couldn't see us."

"Oh." I digested this. "What sort of people?"

"Police. Doctors. His wife. A man taking photographs."

She made it vivid; I could see it all. "Well, Teddy was important. I suppose his death would cause a fuss." A thought came to me. "He wasn't murdered, was he?"

"Oh no. He killed himself all right. Shot himself through the mouth."

I winced. "But why. Was he ill? Sick?"

"Sick? Yes, Teddy was sick all right, but not in the way you mean. No, he was in trouble. And if he was in trouble, then we're in trouble. It's infectious, it spreads."

I nodded. Some people's troubles stay at home with them. But not Teddy's. He was the sort that took other people with him, no doubt about that. Whatever hell he went to (and I never had any doubt he was headed for a hell of some sort), he wouldn't go alone.

"What sort of trouble?" But I was thinking that there was only one sort of trouble Teddy could be in: public trouble. He didn't have a private life, so there would be nothing about a woman, no debts, no private tragedy, just some great miscalculation connected with his career, because that was all Teddy was: a public man.

"I don't know, but I can guess, can't you? Somehow, somewhere along the line Teddy has played a hunch, backed the wrong horse, call it what you like, and it's blown up in his face."

"Mixed metaphors," I said, thinking that, yes, it could be like that, public life was like that, Teddy's sort of public life. "Still, it must have been a pretty big blunder to make him kill himself."

"It would be, wouldn't it, knowing Teddy? Whatever he was, he wasn't a little man."

Empty maybe, but not little. He had a big façade there.

"Do you think we'll ever know?"

"I don't suppose so." Life with Teddy had accustomed us to secrets. He would go out the way he had lived. There was silence between us. Justine wasn't looking at me but out across the river.

"But this isn't what you came here to tell me?" I asked.

"No." She shook her head mysteriously. "It's Teddy's wife, Eva. They've arrested her."

"Why? What for?"

Justine shook her head slowly, without answering. Then she said, "They just took her." She added, "It was terrible."

"It's connected with Teddy's death."

"Oh yes, it must be."

"Perhaps they think she killed him?"

"Oh no. Teddy killed himself all right."

"Then I suppose we know what would have happened to Teddy if he had not killed himself; he would have been arrested."

The wind struck cold off the river now and my thoughts were even colder. I shivered. I looked around; the garden was by no means empty although it was still relatively early in the morning. A woman and a child were walking round the aviary, a woman with a shopping basket crossed behind the trees and a man sat reading a newspaper. Two men were standing by the gate.

"Are you sure no one followed you here?" I said.

"Quite sure. No one followed me. Not interested."
She smiled. "Anyway, they trust me." She did not ex-
pand this statement. Afterwards it occurred to me that
it was both puzzling and alarming. She looked at her
watch. "I'll have to go. I've got Eva's old mother waiting for me. She lives with them, you know. I've taken
her home with me."

"That's good of you, Justine."

She shrugged. "Though she won't stay long. She
wants to get back to the country. You can't blame
her." She went on: "She's quite interesting really. A
real countrywoman. I never thought of Teddy's wife
having that sort of background, did you?"

"Well, she comes from the same village as Anne.
Yes, I did know."

We were walking towards the gate. "I ought to
come and see you," she said.

"Now is not the time."

"I'd like to come and see my father."

"I'm not sure he is your father." I couldn't explain
more to her. Not then.

"No. I'd like to come and see for myself."

"I don't want you two to meet. Not yet." I was
determined to keep them apart. There was danger for
her in a meeting; I didn't know how, but I could feel
it.

There was plenty of danger for us all perhaps with
Teddy dead and his wife arrested. I supposed that
the next time I saw Eva she would be on trial. Or
perhaps she would kill herself before it came to that,
just like Teddy had. I wondered what the charge
would be. Whatever it was, there would be money
involved in it. Money was her great weakness just as
she herself, I supposed, had been Teddy's.

At the gate I said goodbye to Justine. She turned
one way and I went the other. Without meaning to I
began to hurry. I wondered why Justine seemed so
sure of so many things. Why she wasn't followed, for

instance. I ought to have asked myself why she had meekly accepted my ban on meeting her father. The normal Justine would have been round in ten minutes. I see now that she was already deeply concerned for me.

As I passed the block where Anne lived I looked up automatically. I suspected Anne of being a traitor, both personally to me and to the country, but, all right, having loved her for so many years I couldn't now give up. Her windows were wide open with the curtains drawn back. She was standing there looking down. She must have seen me. I thought she leaned forward and waved to me, but I hurried on, pretending not to see. My time with Anne would come, probably, but it wasn't due yet.

I was almost running as I turned the corner away from the river. I crossed the main road at a trot. Straight ahead of me was a grocer's shop, its windows full of tinned food. I knew this window of old; I knew that if you stared into the depths of the window past the tins there was a mirror in which you could see the street behind.

I stood there, getting my breath back and unobtrusively studying the mirror.

Yes, there turning the corner across the street was a stocky figure in a brown suit, one of the two men who had been standing by the park gates. He lumbered across the road, looking rather heavy on his feet. I think it was his feet that decided me; they looked like feet used to following people.

Perhaps Justine had been wrong in believing herself not followed. There had been two men at the park gates. One for her and one for me?

I knew a quick way home. I opened the shop door, walked in, nodded to the boy behind the counter, said: "I'm just going in to see your mother," but didn't and marched through the side passage and right out the back. There was a square yard there, with an opening almost opposite where I lived.

I sprinted across the road, up the stairs, and was in-side my own front door.

Quickly I had my prisoner's gag off and was setting his hands free. I wanted him talking.

CHAPTER FIVE

I wanted him talking, and if possible walking too. Right out of my life. But I didn't have much hope of the latter. Still, he had to be talking, and making good sense.

When the bonds were off, he shook himself like a dog.

"I'm glad to see my first judgment of you was correct," he said ironically. "You are not a woman to let sex influence her actions."

I ignored this. I had half forgotten how I had stroked his arm; when the memory of it came back, it didn't shame me, all I thought was: what a pity, he would now be more on his guard with me and I wouldn't be able to use that weapon again. It was a dangerous, two-edged weapon, anyway; one I was better off without. Unluckily it is a weapon no one is without, even if they think they've put it away, or have forgotten how to use it.

"We must talk."

"You start," he said. "You were the one who broke off when we last began. It's your turn."

"Did anyone call while I was out?"

"A heavy-footed friend of yours came banging in, calling you and talking about soup."

"Antoinette!" I was surprised and alarmed: I did give her a key once. I must get it back. "Is that all?"

"I would like to be able to tell you that the bell and the telephone rang non-stop while you were 'out' as you put it, but as a matter of fact, no."

"I think they will be coming."

He groaned. "I knew it. Why?"

"They've arrested Eva."

"Eva?" Did he or did he not look puzzled? I waited. But he cleared that hurdle. "Oh, Teddy's wife."

Now was this or was this not confirmation of the relationship he claimed? Because Teddy had not been married when my husband disappeared.

"You don't know Eva," I said sceptically.

"She was Teddy's secretary before he married her. You've forgotten that. I knew her before he did."

There was an utter ring of truth about this and I felt sure that whoever he was he did indeed know Eva.

"You must explain that to me some time," I said. "But not now. Teddy's dead and Eva's been arrested."

"You don't know why?"

"I can imagine," I said grimly. "Justine was puzzled. But she didn't know what I know about you. Eva is in your pay."

He laughed. "You think Eva is on my side?"

"Not side. No. Eva doesn't take sides. The only side she's interested in is the one with butter on it. You gave her money. Or you helped her towards material things. She always had more possessions than anyone else. Eva likes that."

"Poor old Eva. You are writing her obituary."

"Teddy's written his. I suppose he was mixed up in it too."

"I think I need a wash after my rest on that chair. I'll just go along and freshen up, as the Americans say." He began to stroll away; he knew how to be insolent as well as me.

"Wait a minute. It might not be as quiet a stay as you imagine. Eva has been arrested. I think *I* was followed."

"We've had the police in before," he reminded me. As if I'd forgotten.

"And when they come again?"

"You'll have to hide me."

"You don't understand," I began . . .

"It is you who do not understand. *You will have to hide me.*" He looked back. "I doubt if you were followed. *You're here, aren't you?*" He sounded contemptuous.

"I said we must talk. *You've* said nothing."

"What I've said, you've understood."

"You've made me understand you think me a liar, and a fool," I said. "I understand that all right. Perhaps I am." He waited for me to go on. "But you haven't explained to me at all why I should dig my own grave for you."

"It won't be your own grave if you're careful."

"I'm careful," I said. "So what? Teddy was careful, and look at him."

"Yes, things are moving," he said thoughtfully. "I'll tell you why Teddy killed himself. I was staying with him before you. Oh yes, Teddy had me before you."

"You stayed with him? In that flat?"

"Perhaps stayed isn't quite the word. He had me, but he didn't know he had me. Oh, he felt my presence all around him. Certain little touches," he said grimly. "But he never saw me. Teddy never saw his inferiors. I was invisible to him. I worked there. I looked after the whole block. I stoked the furnace in winter, put out the garbage and cleaned the windows. I was a very useful fellow. I suppose we passed each other most days, but no, Teddy never saw me.

"He felt my eye upon him and little by little it made him uneasy. But he never knew where it came from. Oh, he was invaluable to me, was Teddy. He showed me things he never knew he showed me, gave me ideas I wasn't meant to learn."

"Poor Teddy," I said.

"Well, he had a lot to answer for, you know. In his past he had tried to hunt with the hounds and run with the hare."

"Perhaps he didn't have much choice," I said bitterly. "Is there ever much choice?"

"Well no, not a lot. But even within the area in

which Teddy had a choice he chose Teddy, first, last, and all the time.'

"And you blame him for that?"

"Not blame him, no, but should I love him for it?" He looked reflectively at his own wrists. "No, there was no escape for Teddy."

So I knew why he was telling me: there was to be no escape for me either.

By now it was almost midday. Then the door bell rang. Two short buzzes. He disappeared at once, leaving me standing alone.

I stood behind the door for a moment while they rang again. No, they weren't going to go away without an answer.

I opened the door and there they stood, my three sweet laughing friends: Anne, Xandra and Catherine; they were laughing and arm in arm. Xandra had a new hair style, very short and straight.

"I waved to you from the window to say I was on my way," said Anne. "But you wouldn't stop."

"You haven't forgotten we were coming?" said Xandra.

"First Saturday in the month," said Catherine. "Our lunch: hope you've got a good one organised, I'm hungry already." Catherine was always hungry. Her pretty round good looks seemed to need an enormous amount of food to keep them going. Nor was she easy to feed: the quality had to be high, bean soup wouldn't do for her. But of course I had nothing to offer them, not even bean soup. And I couldn't let them into the kitchen.

"She's forgotten," said Xandra. "Never mind, we'll help cook." And they sailed forward to the kitchen.

"No, no," I cried, barring their way. "I've got some coffee made, have that first while we talk. And I haven't forgotten. I've got a surprise. We're going out to lunch."

"She's got rich," said Anne.

"No, just across the road, but it'll be a change."

"From your cooking, dear, it will," said Xandra, following me, in spite of my protests, into the kitchen. It was quite empty, he wasn't there. I supposed he was in the cupboard. I hoped he wasn't in the bathroom, because if there was one room my friends were always darting into to check their lipstick and to comb their hair and look at their teeth it was the bathroom. Nervously, I watched them while the coffee heated. But except for Xandra, who stood beside me humming and playing with a knife, they sat down where I told them quite peacefully, Anne talking to Catherine, who was quiet.

"Do put that knife down." I looked out of the corner of my eye. "You're making me nervous."

"Where's that knife I gave you?"

"It's around." It was the knife I had cut myself with.

"I can't see it."

"Thank goodness." I didn't want to see it again myself. Ever.

"What?"

"Nothing." The coffee was steaming. I picked up the tray, the cups wobbling.

"Your hand *is* shaking," said Xandra. She had nerves of steel herself.

"My brother-in-law, Teddy, has killed himself. I've just heard."

"Oh." She made her eyes round.

"Don't say anything to them. Just leave it."

"So," she said, taking the tray from me and carrying it on one hand, playing the waitress. "No wonder your hand shakes." She went on ahead of me.

"She's made the coffee good this time," said Catherine, drinking greedily.

Anne was looking round the room. I wondered if she was expecting to see traces of my visitor. Perhaps I was wrong to suspect her, but she did seem on the alert.

"Oh, I must have some more sugar," said Catherine,

rising to her feet and darting back into the kitchen, carrying her cup. Anne went after her, laughing. "You'll spill it," she said.

They seemed a long while in the kitchen; I followed them out.

Catherine was rattling at the big cupboard door and giggling.

"We think you keep your new-found wealth in here," she said.

"Tug it harder," said Anne, still laughing.

The door did not yield; I can only suppose he was pulling hard on the other side.

"There's a bowl of sugar on the table," I said, keeping my voice cold and steady. I picked it up. "Come on, back into the other room."

"Yes, do," said Xandra from the door.

"Oh, you are all edgy this morning." Catherine was still giggling.

"Oh, come on," said Xandra, giving her a little push.

"Yes, all of you. Stella, forgetting all about us coming this morning—she did, you know. You nagging away like anything. Oh, yes, Xandra, you're in one of your cross moods, all right. And Anne . . ." She turned to look at Anne.

"And Anne?" I too looked at Anne.

"What about me?"

"Oh well, you know how you were when we came in to collect you. Why I've never seen you so excited. I thought you were going to bite my head off. And why? Just because I answered the telephone for you."

"I didn't want to take that call."

"Well, you didn't, did you? No one did. You had the receiver back on in a flash. It's her husband," she announced to the room. "They've quarrelled again."

"We never quarrel," said Anne wearily. "It's never like that."

"Do I smell something burning?" said Catherine, wickedly.

Anne flushed.

"You'll go too far one day, Catherine," said Xandra. "And we'll all turn on you and eat you up. Gobble, gobble."

So Catherine stopped. It was only a game with her, but a game she sometimes played too hard.

Catherine was the one who teased us, Anne was the one who judged us purely and gently by the light of her own integrity, and Xandra was the one who stood apart. And I, what was I? I am ashamed to say that I was the one they played up to. My part was to be the audience; they watched me as they performed.

Xandra watched me alertly. I remained calm.

"Shall we go now?" I said. "It's better not to be too late."

I locked my door behind me carefully and led the way downstairs. The staircase was quite empty, the whole house still and quiet. I looked around as we came out into the street, but this was empty too.

It would have been nice if the restaurant across the road could have been empty as well, but that was too much to hope for. I managed to get a table where I could watch my own windows across the road. By tilting my head backwards I could see Atabi sitting on my geraniums and sunning himself. I drank some water from the carafe on the table. It didn't taste good, they were chlorinating the water too much this summer. Vaguely, I wondered why. I was hot, tired and deeply anxious. Naturally I was a little slow to realise why this table had been empty in a crowded room.

"I'm taking up yoga," said Catherine.

"What for?" asked Xandra.

"Discipline," said Catherine, spreading out her pretty hands. "Criticism. Why don't you do it?"

"I have plenty of critics of my own," I said.

"Me too," said Xandra. "Real professionals."

Now, I was wondering why this table had been left empty. No one wanted to sit at it. Why did no one want to sit at this table? Because the last person who had sat at this table had dropped dead, that was why. We weren't a superstitious society, but they were taking no risks.

Elizabeth, flushed with cooking, came out of her kitchen at the back and told us that the beef was the best thing to eat today.

"With paprika," she said. "You get good paprika in this country. No sour cream, though," she said with a shake of her head. "Or not as it should be." Then she said in a low voice that only I could hear: "This is the table *he* sat at." She looked up across the road. "The last thing he saw must have been your windows. He was watching you. Must have been." She looked at me with a kind of hopeful sentimentality. "Think he was in love with you?" I shook my head. "No? I just thought he might be. He looked like a man in love. Or looking for something."

"I didn't know him," I said, my voice thick. Really he must have looked like a man about to die. Perhaps the look was the same.

"He was a man you felt you knew," said Elizabeth. "Only you didn't."

"That's right." She shrugged. "Oh well, that's how it is. He looked like a man you could know."

"In my experience there are plenty of men like that," called Xandra from across the table.

"Oh, in your experience!" said Elizabeth. "That's vast." She pretended to think Xandra immoral. Perhaps it wasn't such a pretence. She went away laughing to get the food.

"What's she talking about?" asked Xandra.

"One of her customers fell dead."

"Oh." Xandra considered. "Lot of deaths round here lately."

It was my own thought exactly. She must have read it in my face.

"Want to confide?" she asked. The remark went back to an old joke. We didn't tell each other all our secrets, far from it, but occasionally one or other of us would want to confide and secrets thus told were kept for ever. If you didn't use the magic word 'confide' you were apt to find your closest dreams handed round like a much opened parcel.

I shook my head.

"You've got something to confide," she said, giving me a look. "Since when did you use a razor? There's one in your kitchen."

"I once had a husband," I reminded her. I think I abashed her. Anyway enough to silence her for the moment. Probably not for long though. It was impossible to silence any of us for very long.

Across the table Catherine was still talking about her yoga classes. I'm not sure if class was really the right word (although it was the one she used) as there appeared to be only her and one other person at it. Yoga wouldn't last long. Catherine was always taking things up and then dropping them. We all three did it a bit, she more than anyone. It made us, as a group, a little unpredictable.

It shouldn't have been a gay lunch but suddenly it was. We were all talking at once. I looked round at their faces; animated Catherine, beautiful Anne, and Xandra so poised and so made up that she was never quite what she seemed.

Elizabeth brought us fruit and cheese.

"The cheese isn't up to much," she said, giving it a sceptical poke. "The plums aren't so bad, though." She put a fresh plate in front of me. "I've got George outside waiting to have a word with you," she said in a low voice.

"Tell him later," I said.

"He won't like it."

Behind her I could see George's anxious face peering through a door. He nodded and made a face at me. Xandra saw it. "Oh, your boy friend," she said. George hated this description. He heard and glowered at her. I'd never been sure what glowered was before but the moment George glowered I recognised it. "Let him come and sit down and have some ice cream."

On these terms George was willing to come. He sat there licking his vanilla ice cream and waiting his opportunity. It came as Xandra and Catherine debated whether to have cheese or hard plums.

"There's a man looking for you," he said in a low voice. No need to ask how he knew, he had his own undercover world. "I think he's watching you. Perhaps he wants to talk to you. I wasn't sure you'd want to see him."

I shrugged. I thought if he was the man I had imagined to be following me earlier then it wouldn't be long before he found me. He had been watching Justine; it would be easy to identify me as her step-mother.

"I don't think he'll find you just yet," George said, "because you've got your friends round here." His eyes looked at me, big and bold.

"You thought he was the sort of man I wouldn't want to meet?"

"I'm not sure." He was cautious.

"What did he look like?"

"Shortish. Square. Brown suit. I didn't see him too close."

It was probably the man I had seen behind me earlier, but there were plenty of men wearing brown suits that summer. "I think I've seen him," I said.

George nodded and licked his ice cream spoon. He wasn't one for asking questions. He preferred to give information rather than seek it.

"Shall I stay with you?" he said, hopefully. I could see him casting himself as my protector.

"No, I can manage." I didn't want George mixed up in this; he had plenty to worry about in his way of life as it was.

Elizabeth bustled past, giving George a frown. There was always a kind of war on between her and George, whom she both patronised and bullied. She said he was undernourished and on this account she was constantly thrusting bowls of rich soup at him. She had also bought him a great thick winter suit to wear which made him look like a stranger. I think really he was just a boy who was always going to be hungry and awkward and not on terms with this world. Perhaps adolescence would give the coup de grace to this manner and he would sink back into being ordinary. Or he might turn out to be really remarkable. You couldn't be sure yet.

Either way I didn't want him killed on my account, or in any way damaged. So I gave him a smile and rose to my feet. As I had known would be the case, the others had let slip the idea of this being my party and momentarily forgotten me and were gossiping together: they looked up surprised I was still there. I couldn't remember all the times they had behaved the same way; forgotten me and then looked up laughing to draw me back into their magic circle again.

"Going?" said Xandra; she was expertly applying pale lipstick. "Me too. I have a rehearsal. Mustn't be late, mustn't be late for this new director—oh he's a positive dragon."

"I must go too." Catherine gathered up her handbag. "I can hardly walk, I've eaten so much. Yoga is out today. No yoga when full of beef stew."

Anne rose too. She put on dark spectacles, although her face was a mask already. Was Anne the traitor?

I let the others walk in front of me as we went out. Xandra was the best actress but the most honest of us three, Anne the most difficult to know and Catherine the most unpredictable.

"You don't look a bit well, Anne."

"I've been thinking just the same about you. At least, not unwell exactly, but as if you'd had a shock."

"Oh, no shock," I said smoothly. "I'm very happy really."

"Are you?"

Now work that out, I was thinking savagely. See what you make of me being happy.

The nasty thing was, there was a sort of happiness in my heart. I hardly dared admit it, it seemed such a shameless irrational unexpected gleam of happiness. I was too old to be going in for a tender sort of love story and the man was the wrong man and the place was not right. Also, I was terribly frightened.

Outside the house I said goodbye to the others. Xandra was playing with a little toy in her hands. She often came back from abroad with a plaything of this sort; it was as if her hands could not bear to be idle. This time it was a tiny golden ball on a chain and she tossed it idly from palm to palm. It was a pretty bauble.

"You could hypnotise someone doing that," I said, my eyes following the bright ball.

"Oh, I do all the time," she said. "Here, catch." She threw it to me. "You can have it." She knew I too liked toys of this sort.

I waved them goodbye and climbed up to my home. I went in, sat down and waited. Everything was quiet and empty. Perhaps he had gone. "No such luck," I said aloud.

"You mean no such luck, I haven't gone?" he said, as he walked in.

"Where did you hide? Were you in the cupboard?"

"Of course. Nice voices your friends have."

I discovered he was quite serious. "I'm sure they look as charming as they sound."

"Yes, they do really."

"And which of them has the deep rich voice?"

"Xandra. She's an actress."

"I'm not surprised. With a voice like that she couldn't be anything else. And the one with the bell-like little giggle?"

"That's Catherine."

"And what does she do?"

"She's just married."

"Of course. It would be a career in itself to a girl with a laugh like that. Husband important?"

"I think he will be one day," I admitted.

"And the one with a voice like a drink of cold water?"

"That must be Anne," I said with a laugh. It did describe Anne's cold clear logical way of speaking. "Could you hear so much?"

"Everything. But naturally I was trying to."

"Are you certain you haven't met them before?"

"If I am the good con man you take me for, what sort of answer do you expect? I'll say no, and you can believe what you like. No."

"Not once? I'd like to be sure of that."

"You don't trust me."

I laughed, not with amusement. "I trust you now to get under cover quickly. But supposing it had been the police?"

He sat down, looking relaxed and at home. "What I've learnt about you, my dear, is that I can trust you to lie efficiently."

"We might both be asked to use our skills at any moment," I said. I told him of George's story. He nodded. "Handy little fellow," he said. "I could use him."

"Leave George out of it," I said sharply.

"If I can."

"I think you do know one of my group of friends. You must do. I'd like to know which of my friends I owe you to."

I walked over to the table and took a cigarette. I noticed he'd been smoking and throwing the stubs away unevenly smoked. So he was nervous behind that calm front.

Atabi, curled up in the window, greeted me with a loud howl.

"You forgot his lunch."

"I had other things to think of."

"But never mind, I found it for him." Atabi gave him a yellow-eyed stare, not quite approving. It took more than one lunch to make him love you. Although, conversely, you could win his undying enmity just by sitting where he wanted to sit. He was a cat of moods and perhaps his love and his hate weren't so far different. You could say that of a lot of us.

"Oh, you know everything about me. I'm sure you did an investigation on me before you moved in which told you where I keep the cat's food."

"You keep it where it was always kept. In the days before cheap refrigeration (you *still* don't have one, by the way) it was kept on the window ledge outside the kitchen." He pointed. "It's still there."

"I can't afford a refrigerator," I said sulkily. He knew too much about me, far far too much. All these little details that only an intimate could know. I hated him.

"Don't boycott me," he said, giving me a smile. "What is such knowledge, anyway?"

"Only a knife. Pointed at me."

"Talking of knives, where is that handy sharp steak knife you wield so well?"

"Oh, round the kitchen somewhere."

I walked over to the window. The sun had gone behind a bank of dark clouds, without in any way lowering the temperature. "There's going to be a thunderstorm." We get a lot of storms in the summer and a lot of fog in the winter: it's a lovely climate.

He came over and joined me, taking care, I noticed, to stand well back so that he couldn't possibly be seen. "You shouldn't have gone across the road to have lunch," he said conversationally. "Keep well away from that place. I think it is dangerous."

All places were dangerous to me now. Teddy was dead, Eva arrested, and across the road I had sat in a dead man's seat. I put my hands over my face.

"I am sorry," he said with dignity and moved away. I heard him go. Have I said that I have exceptionally good hearing? For some minutes now I had been conscious of hearing sounds from the stairs.

Someone had crept slowly up the stairs from the bottom, pausing several times. That stair-well is a funnel for sound when the temperature is right, and it was right now. Hot air and noise were rising together.

The feet had taken a long pause this last time. I took my hands down and listened. Now they were coming up again. Funny noise like crawling. Not like feet at all. Or, like feet not wearing shoes.

I looked across the room at my visitor, who was sitting slumped on the sofa. He had heard nothing.

Soon the feet would be at my door. They were slower and slower, it was a long pull up, but they came on.

"Someone's coming," I said.

"I know," he said, not looking at me.

There was a thud at the door. I stayed by the window. "This is it."

It came again, hardly a bang or a knock, just a soft noise.

He stood there on the threshold, swaying backwards and forwards. I saw his eyes were brown and deep-set. His face I did not know, but it was young. He seemed to recognise me, and hate flooded into his eyes. He put up a hand to strike me; his blow got as far as my cheek before he fell back.

He just touched me, but it was the touch of a dead man.

CHAPTER SIX

"Did he hurt you?" Stephen came forward.

"He's past hurting anyone." The body gave a perfectly involuntary shake, something more than a shiver and less than a spasm.

Stephen turned the body over. In the back was a spreading patch of blood and a knife. The knife was jammed into the rib cage. I recognised it at once. It was my knife, the steak knife, my present from Xandra.

Stephen recognised it too. "Did you get blood on you?"

That was him, practical as ever.

"No." I was shaking. I couldn't take my eyes off the man.

"Where did he come from?"

"It's my knife."

"I know that. Did you kill him? You had the chance on the way in. He thought you did, he tried to attack you."

But I had a question of my own demanding an answer.

"Why did he come here? Was it to see you? Don't answer: I can see it's the truth. And he was killed to stop him talking to you."

He looked sad. "I don't know why he was killed."

"You were supposed to meet here. Perhaps he had instructions for you. Now that's been stopped."

He said nothing.

"And yet no one is supposed to know you are here except those who placed you here."

Still he kept quiet.

The man in the dark suit with the heavy gold fob, very plain, very beautiful, said savagely: "That was a bad business. He had no business getting killed."

"Yes, I can see you are critical." Brown suit was being tough. "But it was always a risk. He knew he carried an area, like a round pebble, in his back, that someone might want to stick a knife into. We all know it. Sometimes I can feel my own spot. He rubbed the back of his head. "Knife or gun. One or the other."

The man in the dark suit fidgeted with his papers. "Do we know who killed him?"

"I believe so. It's all there. He kept his notes." Brown suit nodded at the papers. "I got them later. Some were on his body. He was the organiser of *her* position there. I myself was too far away at the time. But all the same, he was deeply suspicious of her. He thought she was contra, contra, contra!"

"He thought she might be a triple cross. Crossing us, them, and then us again. Don't you even feel sometimes that she was a little *too* innocent?"

The other grunted. "Grisly," he said.

"He thought she might have the makings of a ruthless woman."

"It all came out," said the older man. "We know what she was. In the end."

They were not friends, these two. Past, education, even looks divided them. There is one sort of good looks that hates another sort. The interrogator was good looking and thought the other, in looks, rather coarse.

"Would you say," said Brown Suit sardonically, "that we have come to the end?"

"I see you haven't got it quite clear. Not quite clear. They've kept one or two things from you. The man who was stabbed was a friend with two faces. Sure he had a message from us to *them*. But we have reason to think he might have two messages. One ours. One definitely not ours. A dangerous message from the national counter-espionage agents who were suspicious but not specific. We couldn't be sure which message he planned to deliver. So he had to be stopped." He shrugged. "Myself, I wouldn't have killed him, but our agent was hasty. Nervous." He grinned. "You can't trust anyone in this business."

I seized on the bitter truth. "Everything is going wrong, isn't it? From the very beginning things have gone wrong. You know it but you don't know where it's coming from. Perhaps you think it's me?" I laughed.

"Shut up. You're still hysterical."

"You've gone on with your plan even although it's gone sour. The man in the restaurant, the first man to die, was one of you, wasn't he? You've known since then how it was. They're all dead, one after the other they're dead. Even you're dead."

I was surrounded by dead men. I had sat in a dead man's chair, been attacked by a dead man, and a man had come back from the grave claiming to be my husband.

He opened the door slightly and listened. Everything was quiet. He shut it again.

"Now we must work out what to do." He was completely calm again, not so much ignoring my panic as superseding it with his own strength. "We can leave him there, sit it out in here, and act surprised when he's found." He was thinking aloud and giving me the benefit of it. "Or we move him."

"I couldn't." I shuddered.

"We can move him a little." He opened the door, listened, then moved on to the landing and looked down the stair-well. I knew what he saw was a deep dark pit.

He turned to me: "Is there anyone on the stairs? Can you tell?"

I shook my head. "I don't know."

He was pale and practical. "Walk down the stairs and find out."

"I can't go out without passing it."

"Never mind. No one will know."

I stared at him dumbly. *I* would know. I was frightened.

Slowly, my head averted, I sidled out of the door and down the stairs. Then I was halfway down the stairs and hearing a cough. It was a cough and Antoinette's voice.

I knew from the cough who she was speaking to: the old man on the ground floor. He had a dry little cough that spoke of hard days. There must have been a time in his life when only with his cough could he risk any overt criticism of events, then the cough had been his relief. Things were better for him now, but he still had his cough.

Antoinette and the old man were standing together by the front door, which was open all day. By leaning over the stairs I could see them silhouetted against the light.

"That George," she was saying. "Always creeping up and down our stairs. I chased him off. We shall have the police in, that's what. If ever a boy was headed the wrong way, that one is. He's always in and out. I mean, anyone might follow him in. And as it was there was a fellow watching him from across the street. Oh yes there was. Unpleasant looking face, too. I never trust men with their hair cropped right short. Hair means something to me, it does." She was a hairdresser. "And short-haired men spell trouble, I can tell you, and I've met some. Some? I've met plenty."

The old man was heard to murmur that George didn't seem a bad boy. He wasn't enthusiastic. He wasn't taking any more sides.

He went in and shut his front door. Antoinette went back upstairs. I waited until all was quiet again and then crept back.

"All quiet," I said.

Stephen nodded. "Let's go, then."

He bent over the body.

"What are you going to do?"

"Only one thing we can do: drop him over the side. He'll go straight to the bottom and be nothing to do with us."

"Wait a minute," I said. "Who killed him?"

"One of your friends." He was almost casual. "Must have been."

"Because of the knife?"

"Only someone who knew you and your flat well could have taken it. That is, if *you* are telling me the truth."

"And if I'm not telling the truth?"

"Then you did it yourself . . . and he was right to hate you."

"Who was he?"

"Someone I have never been quite sure of," he said slowly. "And if I look upset it is because I am wondering *why* he has been killed." He stroked my face as if there might be an answer there.

We stared at each other. I saw that our relationship was like water, it could take shape only as we gave it shape. He neither trusted me nor distrusted me but as he saw I behaved. It was the same for me. So I didn't bother to answer but simply crouched down by the body.

"What is it we do?"

"You lift and I heave."

The body was very heavy, heavy to lift, heavy to move, heavier than I'd expected.

"I can't do it, I can't."

He ignored this as he was prepared to ignore everything that didn't go the way he wanted it. Had my husband, my own husband been like this? I am bound to say that I remembered he had.

I fell back on my heels and covered my face with my hands. But I had helped him enough. The body slithered over the side and then thudded and bumped downwards. The whole house seemed to reverberate to the sound.

Then there was silence. I waited for someone to rush out and find the body. I waited for screams. Nothing happened. No door opened, no one called out. It took me a moment to realise that with the noise of the fall had come the first thunder of the storm. But it didn't make me feel any better.

"Wasn't such a noise after all," he said. "Solid old house this."

A terrible idea came to me and I rushed forward and looked over the side. "The knife, you fool. You left the knife. It's an American knife."

He pulled me back. He pulled me back into the apartment and shut the door behind us. "They're going to find it in a moment, any moment, and when they do, you're going to be here, at home, knowing absolutely nothing about it."

The door was shut and we were closed in there together. It felt as though we would never get out.

Outside in the street the rain was beating down as the thunder clouds pressed low on us.

"There was a bad thunderstorm one night during the war," I said. "I was very frightened. I thought it was bombs or anti-aircraft guns. So it could have been."

"You can't be old enough to remember the war."

"Ten. You can remember a lot at ten. I hated the Germans."

He gave a laugh. I could see tiny beads of sweat on his temple. "I'm not a German if that's what you're hinting. And what was it, if it wasn't bombs?" He was making conversation just like I was. But in our conversation we were dragging out things that really mattered because we were under stress.

"A thunderstorm like I said."

It wasn't a conversation. He was talking, like I was, to prove we were still alive.

"Oh yes." He wasn't listening to me; he was listening for noises downstairs. I didn't tell him but I had already heard one or two noises. I could guess what one must be too. I knew the ways of this house so well.

That thud, followed by another thud, was Antoinette pulling down her windows preparatory to going out, back to her shop to check the day's takings and see the girls cleared up properly. She always made her windows sound like the guillotine going down.

She would be the first one to see the dead man. And Antoinette certainly knew my knife. She had picked it up and admired it. With a sick feeling I remembered that it must have traces of my fingerprints on it.

There were still at least two other things Antoinette always did after closing her windows and as one was putting on her hat I had a minute or two before she emerged.

"I'm going to get the knife," I said aloud. He made no move to stop me; but he nodded with a strange look on his face.

I opened my door and listened. No sound except a distant growl of thunder; the storm was moving south.

I just had time to think about that look on his face and to wonder what he was up to and had got halfway down the stairs when I saw Antoinette's door open. She had been quicker than I expected. She was wearing a hat with flowers on it and carrying a bag; she was humming as she turned to close the door.

If she turned and looked over the stairs as she went forward she would certainly see the body; he was out of my vision but would be well within hers. I could imagine how he was lying there on his face.

For a moment I thought she wasn't going to look, then I saw her stiffen and stop quite still. She tiptoed to the stair-well and looked right down. I waited. Then she turned round and tiptoed quietly back to her front door.

She looked up and her eyes met mine. Silently she

put a finger to her lips, then retreated behind her own front door. I heard it lock.

That was Antoinette for the day. She had seen nothing, heard nothing and would say nothing. While it suited her interests, at least.

I ran back up. The door, left ajar by me, was shut. It was locked against me. I stood on the stairs wondering what to do, then turned round to go back again. But as I turned I saw George's head appear silently round the stairs. He jumped the last two steps and stood beside me. Behind him was the largest boy I had ever seen. He had a huge frame as well as great height. Dark spectacles obscured his face. He stood silently behind George like a nurse or a warder.

George ignored the tall boy and came straight to the point.

"There's a dead man down there on the stairs."

I watched him without saying anything.

"Is it the man in your flat?"

So he had known I had someone there.

I didn't answer.

"Another man?"

Finally, I said, "No."

"I knew you had someone up there."

"I thought you did."

Some day if George didn't watch out he was going to be very alarming indeed. I wasn't quite happy with him now.

"Who's this boy with you?"

"Oh, don't worry about him," said George, nodding his head to the huge figure behind him. "He's deaf."

"Don't be silly," I said sharply. There wasn't much expression to be seen behind the dark spectacles, but enough to tell me the boy was listening. "Of course he hears."

"I mean when I tell him," said George with a smile. Nothing vicious or anything like that, just rather chillingly out of this world.

"Stop acting like an American gangster, George."

"Anyway he wouldn't understand you," said George, his smile still continuing. "You don't talk the way he understands. He's got a way of talking all his own."

The storm had made the staircase very dark.

"Clear out, George," I said wearily. "Just go away and keep quiet. Forget you were here."

"I'll be all right, you know. No one can touch me."

"You're invisible, I suppose."

"Yes," he said. "I've learnt how. It's easy. No one can touch you if you don't want."

"The trouble is, in the end one always wants." George would find out sooner or later that human beings would rather be vulnerable than invisible, that they'd rather stand up and shout "Beat me!" than not be seen at all.

"You don't know half about me."

We had so little time. Already Antoinette and George and his friend knew about the body. Soon the storm would stop and people would start to go out and then the police would be swarming all over the house.

They say they don't arrest you straight away, but leave you waiting, getting more and more frightened until you are ready to confess all. Then one of them comes up to you and is sympathetic and this is the one you talk to, and then another policeman comes and he is the one who arrests you. Under this new improved system they hardly need to be nasty to you at all, you do it all yourself.

"I could move him," said George. "Take him off. You don't want the police to find him."

"Go away."

I had to think what to do and I couldn't with George prancing beside me like a young pony.

"He's dead, George," I said. "Go away."

"I think we'll take him anyway," he said, in a matter-of-fact voice. "He's what we need."

"What do you mean?"

"We've got a tomb, several that would do, in fact. We need a body."

"I don't like talk like that." I was panting. Somehow I couldn't control my breathing.

"No talk."

Breathlessness still choked me, squeezing my lungs, like a giant hand.

"I do have a tomb. Nice set-up, like I said."

It was true that the man needed a tomb; he could do with being buried.

"Don't upset yourself," said George. "Think of it more as a bed for the night."

"He certainly needs a bed," I said. "His last. You couldn't move him."

"No, but he could." He nodded towards his big friend.

"Through the streets? Over his shoulder?"

"It's very stormy."

"But people have eyes."

"I have my car."

"Yes, your car," I said. It was a car but not an automobile; it was a wooden frame on wheels with a hood that the boys had made themselves. We'd got used to seeing them pedalling around in it. "He's big."

"But not too big." No, he wasn't too big, he could be fitted in, and he deserved a burial. Couldn't I think of it like that? That he had a right to a burial. "The car's round the back. In the courtyard." This was a very old house and coaches had once driven under the big arch at the side and into the courtyard. Or that was what we told ourselves.

I looked down at George, whose head now came up to my shoulder, and I'm tall; he'd been growing lately. I looked in his face. I'd been thinking of him as a child. All this time I'd been thinking that he'd gone through all the experiences of his life and emerged a child, a wild child sometimes, but still a child. It wasn't true. I don't know what he was exactly, but he wasn't a child.

This unchildlike creature and I looked at each other. I don't know what his motives were in helping me, not what he'd told me, I suppose, but he was willing to help.

"I accept, George," I said.

"The first few minutes will be the worst," he said, in a low voice. "As we move him down the stairs and out the back to the car. If we survive that, we're all right."

He knew all about survival.

I followed them slowly down the hill, the car going in front with George behind pushing, and the big boy walking by the side. We passed one or two people but George was known in this district and no one took much notice.

The storm was lifting, a golden colour was appearing in the sky; a burst of sunlight suddenly fell on me; we were going to our burying through a rainbow. This was where the rainbow ended.

We were moving down a steep cobbled passageway. Suddenly I knew where we were going.

In the first century of the Christian era a group of prosperous Roman traders had settled on an area of the town just outside the main walls, but close to a busy road, as their cemetery. They were a well-off privileged community and had built a series of handsome tombs. But as the centuries turned the Roman Empire broke up, the traders left and first the city became Christian, then pagan, then Christian again, and grew and grew. The earth level was raised around the cemetery and then it was built over. These first buildings were superseded by others so that earth and stones and bricks multiplied over the ancient site. Finally, in the war, the bombing uncovered for the first time for over a thousand years a Roman sarcophagus. It was ornate and charming, covered with little birds and cupids, and had been shaped for a child. The whole area was tunnelled into in a careful but limited way; for built above part of the old cemetery was now a famous Gothic church and no one wanted to knock that down.

The church was looming up in front of me now, looking as churches so often did in this part of the town, a little neglected and more than a little dirty. The stone, which once, I suppose, must have been pearly white, was now a deep grey.

There was a proper entrance to the excavations, but it was boarded up and dusty, no one came this way now. In any case, the boys had their own entrance.

So this was it. This shallow tunnel lined with grey cement was the way to the burial chambers.

"Must have been an old air raid shelter once," whispered George. "Nothing now. But we dug a way in through the back to the Roman tombs." He spoke with pride.

It was dark inside and the big one took off his spectacles. He must have had African blood mixed up with something else because he had a strange dark skin and big brown eyes. In spite of his huge frame he was only a boy, as I could see now his spectacles were off. He looked right through me without expression, seeming not to see me. He swayed a little.

"Is your friend sick, ill?" I asked George.

"Sure, sure," he said cheerfully. "He's sick. Been that way a long time."

"He can't stand up."

"He never falls over. Just a little way this way, a little way that."

"Like a dance. But it's worrying."

"When he was little in Cuba something fell on his head and it does something to him."

"Oh, so it's Cuba he comes from." It helped to explain his appearance. Many bloods had mixed in him.

"Yes, Cuba. You can't be that size and not have something," said George philosophically.

"What's he doing over here?"

"Student."

He looked less like a student than anyone I had ever seen.

All the time we were talking we were working with our hands, moving the limp body from the car. Big friend picked it up, not lightly, even he couldn't pretend the weight was negligible, but with confidence. We went through a wooden door they'd fixed up, stumbled down two steps, and found paving stones under our feet.

I looked around me. We were in the city of the dead. I hadn't realised it was so much a little town. The old Romans had built their tombs in the style of tiny shrines and temples and aligned them in streets. You could walk along a narrow paved way with gutters in the middle and look at the monuments on either side. I suppose the area covered was small in fact, but in this dim light coming from only one or two gratings the streets of tombs seemed to stretch into infinity. Over everything was a strange sweet old smell.

"Nice place," said George.

"Yes."

"The Romans made it." He sounded proud, as if the Romans had been close relations. We were standing by the tomb of the Marcii. A printed slip stuck into the wall supplied this information. Judging by their well-found tomb, constructed of narrow red brick with a stone lintel above the door, the Marcii had been a rich family. Not patrician perhaps, the tomb was more than a little ostentatious, but after all they were only traders. Facing the tomb of the Marcii was the lovely mausoleum dedicated to Felicitas Hermes. She and her sisters were buried here together.

Of all the tombs, this tomb of Felicitas Hermes was the most like a little house. A light shone inside.

I knew this place; I knew it much better than I'd let George understand. After all, my husband was an archaeologist and the way I'd met him had been at a dig. Not *this* dig; but this site, although neglected now, had been relatively new and exciting when I was a student and we had visited it. We had felt we were on the edge of new discoveries, perhaps we should discover a whole Roman city. But no more discoveries turned up and gradually the cemetery fell out of fashion. I hadn't heard it spoken of for years.

The three of us moved into the tomb of Felicitas Hermes. The fourth member of the party we left outside. The light had come from a single candle, which was placed on a kind of marble table, which I suppose must have once served some purpose in the memorial rites for the dead. Probably a commemorative meal was served here once a year on the anniversary of the day Felicitas had died. The Romans, like the Egyptians, were much concerned with the material needs of the dead soul.

A group of boys were standing by the table.

"Peter," said George, indicating one after the other, "Edward. John." Each boy acknowledged the introduction with a slight bow. George didn't introduce the rest.

Too many of them to hold a secret, I thought. I could see disaster coming from that minute.

George went over and spoke to them in a low voice. He must have been telling them that he had a body to bury, but there was no sign of alarm or amazement from them.

He came back. "They don't help," he said. "We do it alone. But they agree."

"Did you have to tell them?"

He looked surprised. "This is their place, too. It's a good place. We may need to live here one day." I suppose he saw the look on my face. "In the next war. Or in the revolution," he added in a matter of fact way. He never doubted there would be a war or a revolution.

We withdrew outside the tomb of Felicitas Hermes.

The street of tombs was darkly shadowed. The big boy stepped forward into a patch of darkness, George followed, then me.

In the dusk, scented with old stones and dust made of still older things, they showed me a stone sarcophagus.

"Here," said George. "He can lie here."

Yes, there was a smell of death over this place.

"It is a good box. It will do him honour."

He held up a torch for me to see the sarcophagus. It was big, constructed of pale creamy stone, now turning amber in places, and much scarred. Enough remained of the original decoration for me to see that on one side was a military procession. On the other side were the Four Seasons with fruit baskets representing the endless circle of life. The lid showed two roughly decorated figures, both soldiers surrounded with corn sheaves and laurel leaves.

It was a soldier's tomb. I suppose in a way *he* was a sort of soldier. He was a casualty of war, whether he knew it or not.

The knife had come out, but I buried it with him anyway.

As we turned to go we all heard the noise at the entrance. The candle light at once went out. George and Peter seemed to disappear, although I thought I could hear them breathing not far away. Then this sound too disappeared.

I heard a light purposeful footstep.

I had time as the noise drew nearer to work out what it was.

Earlier today I had been followed. Someone, probably this same follower, had been asking about me; George thought he had put him off. He was mistaken. For a little while I had equated the man asking questions with the man stabbed at my door. In this *I* was mistaken. There were two men. The relationship between them (if there was one) was unclear.

Perhaps my pursuer had even known about the

murdered man. But forget that. It was reasonable to assume he had been hanging about and had seen our procession set off.

Now he had caught up with me.

I could hear his tread coming nearer. I couldn't see him but I could hear him.

Behind me I heard George moving about; I felt him give me a little tug, trying to pull me further back into the darkness.

The man was walking lightly and carefully but he didn't know the way about this necropolis; I heard him stumble and swear. I couldn't identify the language. It wasn't English, American or Russian. Or was it? Sounds bounced off these walls and echoed back in your ears.

My eyes were more used to the dim light now. I was standing in a recess of a broken tomb looking down the main street of the necropolis.

The man stumbled and caught hold of a piece of masonry to steady himself. Perhaps, the odd thought came to me, he didn't have very good eyesight. His figure, short and slight, was just visible in the gloom. He seemed to carry a light of his own with him.

A piece of masonry rattled down where he had pulled at it and fell near him. He was within arm's reach of me now. Reaching out I grabbed a large object, it could have been some sort of lustral vase, and struck him. He sagged. I hit him very hard once more and then again. He slid down in front of me.

The questioner, or interviewer, as he could be called, was a slender man clearly at the peak of his professional life. The muscles of his face were flexible and well used, almost as if he had come into his present career through the stage. You felt that he was well versed in pretending to be what he was not. Beside him, the other man appeared a monster of straight-forwardness.

"Who was the man she hit? You, I suppose?"

The man in the brown suit nodded. "I'll always have a scar," he said morosely. "I was a fool to let her get near me. But that place, that cemetery, threw me off. You've no idea what it was really like down there. It smelt."

"Not up to your usual standards. You did better with the fire in Hamburg. In those days you were good."

"This time we were operating under pressure."

"You were shot up, you mean," said the other man sourly. "You let her throw you."

"I got burnt in that fire in Hamburg." He rubbed his cheek reflectively.

"I think you got burnt again. She weakened you. Did you like her looks?"

Clearly they were not men who could ever come to like each other.

"I did the best I could. At least I didn't give her any comfort. Didn't let her guess what was really happening to her."

He was polite, affable, turning, yet insolently, the other cheek. But that's the business.

I don't know when I first realised that the boys were quarrelling among themselves. Dazed by the whole situation I had at first thought of them as a completely harmonious group. Now I saw that they were not so. Instead, they fell into two factions. My friend George was a leading figure in one group. The other had the boy called Peter for leader. They were edgy and aggressive. I felt a little betrayed by George for leading me into a situation he could not properly control.

The ostensible cause of the quarrel was something very trifling, the ownership of a small digging instrument, something like a trowel, only with a longer handle.

"That's mine," said Peter. "Mine, Tot."

"No one's. Belongs to no one," said George. He was an anarchist.

Suddenly the quarrel seemed to flare up again and before I could stop them they were in combat. Hardly unarmed combat, either. Each boy had a brick or a stone.

"Stop it, you fools," I shouted.

There were two parties forming before my eyes and the battle was over possession all right, but not then of the trowel. They were fighting for territory.

But they hadn't quite realised what had happened to them. They were fighting over lost territory. They had given it up to the dead.

Before George could really get into the fight, I had a grip on him and pulled him away. He resisted a little, but not too much. Open combat like this was not his way; he was more of a secret fighter. Besides, he and I had other things to think about.

On the floor was an unconscious man. In the tomb was a murdered one. I wondered if they'd find each other.

"Shall we kill this one?" whispered George. He could ignore the gang fight and concentrate on mine. Although a highly possessive person, he had been deterritorialised a long time ago. He was the human snail (the type we're breeding now) with his world on his back.

The man on the ground moved his eyelids slightly, as if he might come round.

"I'll know your face again," I said viciously.

"Is he a friend or an enemy of the man we buried?" asked George.

"I don't know."

"Is he your friend?"

"He can't be, can he? If there's sides, then he and I are on different ones."

"Yes." George nodded. He knew all about sides.

"What did Peter call you?" I asked, remembering something.

"Tot. I'm little, see. We all have our names. Special names."

"And that huge boy, what do you call him?"

"We call him Tanker."

"Does he like that?"

"No, he don't like it. I don't like Tot. But that's his name."

"Who gives you these names?"

"Oh the gang does."

"But you've got two gangs here, haven't you?" I said.

"Yes. But we are allies."

Allies and sometimes enemies, I thought.

"And do the gangs have names?" I asked.

He hesitated. This he didn't wish to tell me. Finally he said, but with pride, "Yes. We're the Roman Emperors."

"That's a good name." I looked around the cemetery. "Especially here."

"Yes, it's good. I'm a Caesar."

"What's that mean?"

"I'm a war lord."

I looked at him. He meant it seriously, I could see. And having seen them in action I took it seriously, too.

"And the other gang," I said. "What are they called?"

"The Big Cats."

"That's not such a good name." My turn to be serious.

"They haven't got much imagination in that lot."

"But good fighters."

"Oh yes. Good fighters. Wait."

George bent down and with quick wicked fingers searched the unconscious man. He found no papers. Nothing except a photograph of a Pekinese dog.

"She is cleverer than you think." The conversation in the room high over the river was still going on. "Did the boy George tell you all this?"

"The boy? No, I got nothing from him. No. I remember the words myself. I was coming round."

"She made a shrewd diagnosis of your relationship," said the interrogator.

"Was she honest? That was the question that plagued me," mused the other man. "How far could I trust her? Could she be made to love the man I had planted on her?"

"There were other ways of putting her under control."

"Suggest one. No. It was a good idea. I had her halfway there."

He was a hard line behaviourist. Put a character in X position under Y influences and the character should produce XY reaction. You ought to be able to measure it. But life constantly reminded him that other factors existed; characters bust out and walked away acting different parts from those assigned.

"I think she's a clever woman," persisted his superior. "She's already set up a relationship with you, whether you like it or not." He was a product of the Humanist traditions and believed that even Pavlov's dogs influenced Pavlov's life. You weren't really outside the cage with your performing animals, but in there with them waiting to do your turn.

"You won't be able to come back here," I said. George and I were standing at the entrance to the tombs. I don't know where the others had gone. A long way away, I hoped.

"Might be able to," said George. He wasn't giving anything up. "Depends. Will he know what hit him?"

"I hope he'll think it was a stone he brought down on himself. With the sort of concussion he's got he may not have too good a memory of these last few moments."

"You're a puzzle, George." Now we were walking back through the streets, and the rain had stopped and people were beginning to come out. I knew I had done wrong to let George help. I had given him a pair of boots for his birthday and in return he had done this for me; it wasn't fair exchange.

"I saw. I wanted to help."

"You saw?"

"I saw you kill the man."

"Tell me what you saw."

"I saw you standing there on the stairs just above me."

"How did you know it was me?"

"I saw your pink dress."

"Does it look like this dress?" He shrugged. To him it did.

I had suspected for some time his sight was poor. He stared about him sometimes like a short-sighted person.

"You know too much about the world, George," I said sadly. "I can't protect you or help you. You know it all."

He smiled.

CHAPTER SEVEN

My front door opened easily to my touch, swinging forward as soon as I turned the handle. This time Stephen didn't want to lock me out.

I advanced into the room. It was tidy and empty. From where I stood I could see straight through into the kitchen. No one there. I walked forward and looked into my bedroom. No one there.

He had gone.

The strange wind of circumstances, which had blown this man who claimed to be my husband into my life, appeared to have blown him out of it again.

Atabi leapt from his seat in the window and came towards me purring. It was an old cat's purr, thick and deep in his throat. I bent to stroke him. A few tears came into my eyes. I was crying for myself alone.

I turned back to close the door and there he was. Silent. Watching.

"You've been there all the time."

"I had to see if it was you. And who you were with."

"I am with no one."

"No." He stepped forward into the room. The now usual feelings of anger and trust which he aroused in me sprang up at once.

"You were crying."

"Not for you. Before you came into my life I had a day, a life in front of me."

"We've been into this before. I've been in your life a long long time."

"So you say."

"And what about—" He checked himself, as if he

had been going to say a name. "What about the body?"

"I buried him. Only temporarily, I expect he'll be found."

He listened while I recounted. He was a good listener, but then he had to be, it was his trade. I was a good visualiser, that was *my* profession, and what I could see now was the picture of my fantastic procession going through the streets and somewhere behind it the follower.

I told him about the other man. He took it all without comment. Words were indeed superfluous. I had acted. For better or worse I had done it. But somehow he knew about the man. He had heard of him. Even met him. I was certain of it.

It seemed to me that remotely in time I could hear my long dead grandmother saying bluntly, "Daft. Plain daft, that's what you've been."

"The dead man may stay buried. Not a bad end, to be buried like that. He was lucky."

"George thinks I killed him."

"Why?"

"He saw me kill him."

"Does he say so?"

"Yes. He says he saw a woman in a pink dress lift her hand to stab. He had to hide himself then because he heard a noise, and when he came back she'd gone." I added deliberately; "He didn't see me, of course. But he saw a woman with a dress something resembling this. Anne was wearing a check linen skirt with plenty of pink in it, Xandra was wearing a dress printed in roses and Catherine was wearing a pink linen suit. You can take your pick."

"I will."

"Yes. Do. And of course, it's why the man tried to attack me. As he died, he thought I had killed him. It's a pretty picture, isn't it?" I suppose my voice was rising, it felt as if it was rising, and I rather liked the feel of it. Something inside me was getting fed by it.

"How many creatures are there now that have got to stay buried? What's the number? Let's tot up the score. First, the man in the cafe opposite. Second, Teddy. Third, the American. I am presuming he was an American. He looked Anglo-Saxon. Then there is the man who drowned in the river near Anne's house a few weeks ago, perhaps he was another? Will they all stay buried?"

"You didn't kill him."

"Thanks. Big thanks."

"I don't say you couldn't kill someone, probably you could. Most people could in the right circumstances."

"And what would constitute the right circumstances?"

"For most people, the need to protect themselves. For you, I think rather the need to protect someone else."

"I have no one else."

Atabi got up and walked slowly across the floor. I watched.

"Justine?"

"What makes you think I may have to protect Justine?" I still watched the cat.

"Because you'd do it. She's your one vulnerable spot, you ought to know it, and sooner or later that always comes up for auction."

"You're wrong." I stood up. "I've got any number of vulnerable spots. And I've got them all paid for. It took ten years of my life, but I did it."

"I don't think you've killed anyone. But one of your friends killed the man to protect you."

"It's like a detective story, isn't it? We have three suspects. Which one is guilty?"

He was warning me about Justine, of course. I could see the warning, but unfortunately I misunderstood it. Darling Justine.

Time was getting very short, but I hadn't at that moment a true notion of time. I thought it stretched out on either side of me, past and future. What I didn't see was that the past was rapidly catching up to the future and going for a ride with it. And then again, I was rather inclined to think of there being a past, my past, and another past that was someone else's, a past for everyone. Whereas of course they were all mixed up together.

"What were you doing while I was away? Why did you lock the door against me?"

He was silent.

"I believe you were searching. Or hiding something. It must have been one or the other. Which was it?"

I began to walk about. Atabi and the man sat watching me.

Everything looked the same. If he'd been searching, he'd been neat. But he would be.

Atabi knew the answer, but I hadn't managed to teach him how to speak. I bent down and patted his head. He was pleased and rubbed himself against me. Then he went over and rubbed himself against Stephen.

"You've been feeding him."

"It is always a good thing to be on friendly terms with the animals," he said with a faint smile.

I made a decision. I'd been making them all day now, right and wrong.

"I think I'd like to find out more about the figure from out of my past, this friend who tells you so much about me, and who uses my knife. I'm going out to call on Xandra, Anne and Catherine."

"Will they be home?"

"Never mind." I could find them if I had to; I knew their habits. A thought came to me. "*You* must know which of my friends is your informant."

"Unfortunately no. We communicated through a third party."

"Then ask this third party."

"Also dead." His eyes met mine. He added, "More or less, anyway."

"They're wiping out the lot."

"Perhaps. I don't know. They may be getting assistance."

"Who from?"

"From people's own guilt. Fears. Their own carelessness." He sounded angry.

"Teddy." I saw by his face I was wrong. "Teddy's wife. *She's* been the intermediary. For money, I suppose. More fur coats and those nasty jewels. The money had to come from somewhere. And Teddy found out. That's why he killed himself."

Perhaps it wasn't the entire story, but it was a convincing beginning.

"I think I shall call on my friends."

"You're tired."

"Not so tired."

He was treating me like a wife. I was behaving like a wife now. As soon as he said I was tired, I *felt* tired, but I contradicted him all the same. Then he told me it was a waste of time to go. That was the way to make me go on.

"I think I know you now," I said, taking up a worldly stance. "Run for cover if you must while I'm out."

I have this gift. Or perhaps it's not as straightforward as that, perhaps it's not a gift, perhaps I am just very aware of what lots of people do without realising it. I'm a sensitive. Oh, I don't mean I can read unopened envelopes or clear someone's mind with a glance. But I know how to get what I want from my friends. I can sense an area of response and press forward. Words form in my mind. Pictures, too. (Strong emotions, such as I felt when I looked at Stephen, can block this.)

Still, I had a way with my friends. I didn't try to force a rhythm out of them nor would they have stood for it if I had, but I could if I tried get them to speak what was on their minds.

It came out in a curious literal kind of way rather like a psychologist doing a reaction test. What I got was what they could not keep back.

I didn't do it very often. The last time I had done it had been when there was no news of my husband and when I thought they might have heard and they weren't telling me. As it turned out Xandra did know something: on her travels she had heard from a journalist about an archaeologist who had been killed by nomadic tribesmen. This was my first intimation of the story that was afterwards confirmed.

The two men in the big stuffy room over the river were still talking.

"*Can* she do this thing?" said the superior. The one who asked the question and wanted an answer.

"I have heard she has some sort of special gift. Not easy to explain. Maybe she's kidding herself a little."

"She's not straightforward."

"Minds can be manipulated. Any common fortune-teller has a shot."

"But can she really do it?" persisted the other.

His companion shrugged.

Xandra had introduced the story: Teddy had confirmed it.

"Wait." Stephen moved away as silently and neatly as the cat, who followed him.

He turned bearing a cup of coffee, hot but not too hot. I could drink it straight away.

"Wait again."

He returned again with some bread and butter. Atabi did not return and was presumably getting his in the kitchen; he liked butter if not bread.

"There are no rules to this situation, are there?" I said. "Here am I, here are you, and I'm drinking coffee. Tomorrow is Sunday and on Monday I have to go back to work and make a film about puppets in a fairy story."

"We are under siege, remember," he said. "And when under siege, eat."

I drank the coffee; he had made it good, strong and hot. He knew I didn't like sugar.

"You are behaving—" after a pause, he added, "well." It was almost a word of praise. Not quite though; an admonition was there as well. Keep it up, he was saying to me.

"I'm not behaving at all. I'm just trying to get through this whole and in one piece." All along a strange fatalism had been within me. "You'll leave here when you want to, I suppose. But don't think I'm not trying to think of ways to get rid of you, because I am."

"That's the spirit." He showed a reluctant admiration. "It's what they said of you."

"What did they say of me?"

"They said that you were reliable."

So they said I was reliable, these unknown traitorous friends. They were real enough, these friends, but no friends to me.

I looked in his face, wondering what I could recognise there. Would I one day look at him and cry out Yes, Yes, it's so. You were not telling me a lie. You are my husband? But he looked tired and a little anxious and more unknowable than ever.

"Don't turn against me," he said. "You and I have a long way to go together."

CHAPTER EIGHT

I walked through the city of which I was potentially, and apparently whether I liked it or not, the betrayer. This city had been created by a society of which I was never quite a part. For a long time I had wanted to be part of it, for some time I had supposed I was, but now I knew it had never been so. Still, strangers do not have to be betrayers. Better if they are not. So I wasn't pleased with my part.

The city was beautiful tonight. The rain had stopped, the street lights were shining on the river and the trees. I was on a bridge. I leaned over and looked in the river. I imagined I could see the city reflected in it. All roofs: we seemed to have more roofs than anywhere else. An old city of roofs and steeples.

A man had drowned in this river not long ago. They said that once you fell in it was impossible to get out. I moved away and walked on.

I was on my way to see Anne.

She opened the door to me herself.

"Hello, Annie."

She raised her eyebrows slightly at that. I didn't call her Annie very often; there was a slight aggression, which she felt, in my doing so now. But Anne had plenty of aggression of her own to match it, if it came to that.

"I'm alone," she said, holding the door no wider.

"It's not really a social call." I had thought out what I was going to say.

"No?"

"You didn't really think it was?"

"You have a look on your face."

I rolled my golden toy in my hands. Anne's eyes followed it.

"It's one look laid on another, really," she continued. "Too many looks. I can't get to the bottom of them."

"No need."

"Oh, there's a need," she said sharply. "But I can't do it."

"Let me be the judge of that." I was still letting my glittering object revolve.

"But you want to be jury as well." She wanted to stop herself saying that, but it was in the front of her mind and she couldn't stop it coming out, feet first.

She led the way into her sitting room. I followed her and sat down.

"Cigarette?"

"Thanks." I was taking my time; mustn't go too fast.

"I used not to smoke so much," she said suddenly.

"I know."

"I know you know." This sort of conversation could be quite ludicrous sometimes.

I was silent, to give her a chance to keep quiet, but she wouldn't.

"You're dressing better these days."

"Well, I have more money."

"No, it's not that, you're choosing better." She looked in my face, a long look. "What a beauty you are, Stella, but it took you a long while to believe in it, because you didn't look like us."

"You're making me feel quite glum."

"No need. It's the bones. Yes, you have better bones."

"Thank you."

"Oh, no need for thanks. Who thanks you for the truth?" She was getting reckless.

"I would."

"No. You only think you would."

"Well, some of the truth anyway." No point in getting impatient with her.

"That's better."

We two knew each other so well. I saw her mouth droop and knew she was miserable.

"How are you, Anne?" I said. "Tell me how you really are. Unhappy?"

This was where she was weak to my pressure. And why? Because she needed to talk about herself.

"I've just come through a bad patch in my work," she confided suddenly. "I feel better about it now. But for a time I thought I was stuck. I can't afford that in my line of work."

"I've never been sure what you were working on," I admitted. "I know the general field, of course."

"Oh, neurology is so technical," she said. "If I'm too precise you wouldn't understand. But all my ideas seemed to be contradicting each other. I *was* in a state. There was a man too. A colleague, you know." Her voice trailed off. I didn't pursue this point, I didn't want her private loves and hates.

"I was glad to see you today, Anne."

"Well, I didn't think you were," she said. "Any more than I was glad to see you." The trouble was that although there were all sorts of rivalries and tensions between us, we were all fond of each other. Left to ourselves we might have had a deep tranquil set of relationships, the sort our great-grandmothers had when a girlhood friend was a friend for ever. But our generation had not left us alone.

Her face looked as if she might cry. There was a lot of emotion hidden away inside Anne. She wasn't moody, but she could be very very hard to read.

"I was glad but a little puzzled, Anne," I explained. "I thought you hadn't been quite yourself lately."

She blinked at me and my golden ball.

"Had you?"

"I always act a little. I don't think I've been much different," she said.

"I *was* a little surprised to see you all today. Of course I had forgotten it was my turn to entertain you all. I thought it had lapsed anyway. We haven't really been very regular lately, have we? Whose idea was it to come? Was it yours?"

"No." She laughed.

"Xandra's then?"

"I don't know. Xandra and Catherine just appeared on my doorstep. I didn't wan't to come. I was busy. Perhaps it was Catherine. She gets very bored, I know. She clings to the idea of regular meetings more than the rest of us."

"Xandra was always more your friend than mine," I observed.

"Not any longer. No, I'd say you were closer to her now than anyone. But what am I saying?" She shook her head. "No one's close to Xandra. Not really. Are they?"

But I was asking the questions; not answering them. "Do you mind?"

"No. Once perhaps. But it's happened naturally."

I glanced round the room. She had been working, books and papers were scattered about. Since lunch time she had changed and was now wearing a tweed skirt and blouse. The room looked peaceful enough, the room of a scholar, but Anne's face looked haggard. I couldn't see any sign of her husband. Perhaps this was one of their periods for living apart. My thoughts must have appeared very closely on my face, for Anne smiled.

"He's just away from home for three months. Collaborating with a German on some opera project. The work has to be carried out in Germany because they have the singers there."

I wondered if he'd ever come back. From Anne's voice I got the impression he might not.

A grand piano took up a great deal of space in the room. Anne went across and played a few chords.

"He's left his piano," she said. "He'll be back."

"It looks a valuable one."

"Oh yes, he's a very fine pianist. I think myself he'd

have made a better pianist than a composer. He studied for a few years at the Conservatoire. He still has a divided allegiance."

"But not you?"

"No, not me. I've always been single-minded."

Yes, that was Anne. She's always known what she wanted.

"I respected you very much when we were students," I said thoughtfully.

"Not so much now?" She smiled.

"Well, you know how it is. One changes, develops different standards. I'm not all so much of a piece as you are. Do you remember you and me going to political meetings when we were students?"

"I remember," said Anne.

"Have you talked to anyone about it, Annie?" The diminutive came spontaneously.

"Oh yes," said Anne. "I mean anyone who asked me I suppose I'd tell."

"I thought so," I said sadly.

"Xandra and Catherine were talking about it at our last meeting. The time you didn't come."

"I ought to have come." I didn't keep the bitterness from my voice. Anne heard it and threw it back at me.

"You've missed a lot lately."

"*Now* I know it."

"We've all changed without knowing it. You most of all."

"And you?"

"Me least of all."

She got up and walked to the window. I sat quietly, waiting for her to come back. There were some more questions to ask. Presently she came back.

"Anyone there?" I asked.

"No."

"Expecting anyone?"

"I often get up and look out of the window. It's just a habit I have." She was watching the golden ball again.

"Yes. I've noticed. I looked up this morning and saw you. Did you see me?"

"Yes, I saw you."

Her face was very white.

"Anne, do you know why I have called now?"

"No, I don't know."

"Anne," I said sternly, "that's not true." You had to sound like a schoolmistress; it was part of the treatment.

"You came to ask a lot of questions."

"I want to know about a knife. A sharp knife Xandra gave me. Do you know the one I mean?"

"I may know." She was answering more and more slowly.

"You saw it. In my kitchen. I've lost it. Someone took it. Have you seen it?"

She looked perplexed, seeking for an answer. She felt she had to answer, but she didn't quite know what to say.

I waited.

"I saw it in your kitchen."

"Yes. After that?"

"The last time I saw it was on your kitchen table," she said in a mechanical voice.

"Did you see it when you came today?" I persisted. "Are you sure you didn't?" She could have picked it up and used it to kill, was what I thought.

Her telephone rang, her eyes jerked round to it and she stood up. Performance over for the day.

"Did you touch it? Did you see anyone touch it?" I asked, but I knew I wouldn't get anything and I didn't. All she did was to glide over to the telephone and start to talk to her caller in a calm voice.

She waved me goodbye from her desk cheerfully, without interrupting her call, as if there had never been any conversation between us except what a nice evening and how well you look.

And indeed, from her point of view now, there hadn't.

The interview with Catherine was a farce from the word go. To begin with her husband was home and her child and her mother and her mother's second husband. Five people at home and not one of them in the mood to submit to hypnotism. I think they must have been having a quarrel.

Catherine looked hot and flustered and the little girl was crying. Catherine's mother was sitting in a chair drawn up to a table with her lips pressed firmly together, a habit I remembered she had. She nodded and smiled when she saw me. She'd always liked me.

"Tell this silly girl," she said, "not to stand in her husband's light." She herself had never stood in either of her husbands' lights, instead she had inexorably pushed them closer towards it than they could bear, which perhaps explained why both had looked a little dazed. As a young girl I had thought that Catherine's father had blinked and looked short-sighted all his life, but I think now that he had only got that way. The second husband I hardly knew, but I saw he was wearing dark glasses.

Catherine's husband came forward and shook my hand; he was always rather formal. He was a tall, slim young man with possessive eyes. All the group found him difficult. I've always thought he resented our relationship with his wife and the fact that, in many ways, we knew so much more about her than he did.

"Mother!" said Catherine.

"Here he is with this wonderful chance, this splendid promotion, and you say you won't go."

"I don't want to go and live in Timbuktu."

"Not Timbuktu? It's a capital city."

"Very sunny," put in Catherine's stepfather, his expression shielded by his dark glasses.

"Away from all this fog," said her mother.

The baby started to cry.

"Anyway, I don't see where the promotion is," said Catherine. "A nasty climate and not much money. Where's the promotion in that?"

"It's where it might lead," said her mother.

"I know where it might lead." Catherine rocked her daughter, who looked over her shoulder fiercely, unmistakably her father's child.

Catherine's husband stood up. The women in this family did all the shouting, but I ought to have remembered that the men took the important decisions.

"Catherine will like it when we are there," he said. "In any case we don't go for six months. There is plenty of time to talk." He took the baby from her.

"Let me get some coffee," said Catherine, smoothing her hair. "We were just having some." She seemed to accept the idea that I'd come all the way out to their remote suburban flat just on a social visit. But I saw her husband give me a curious look. "It's ages since you've been here and you've hardly seen baby."

"I'm taking her off to bed now," said her husband.

"Yes, she really needs to go," said Catherine, but without bothering to look. "I told you not to get her up."

"She was crying," said her mother.

"And I don't blame her," said Catherine. "I feel like crying myself."

They were off again. I thought there was no point in staying. Catherine seemed so exactly what she was, a harassed and not particularly happy young wife and mother. She seemed years and years younger than me, as though I had grown up and matured and she had stayed exactly the same.

Catherine's mother poured me some coffee and offered me some cake. She had always been a hospitable woman.

"I made it," she said. "Well, we haven't seen much of you lately. I always say to Catherine that it's nice the way you girls keep up with each other, but the last time I spoke she said you didn't see all that much of each other now and she thought it was breaking up."

"It is, I think."

"Pity. Still, there it is, life changes you, doesn't it?

But you've all been very lucky girls and done well. Except your husband, my dear. I didn't mean that," she patted my hand apologetically. "That was real bad luck. Worse things have happened, though, haven't they, dear? Oh yes, the ice has been very thin at times, and we've all skated over it. Look at him, my dear," and she nodded towards her husband. "He hasn't always liked what he's seen, but he's had to put up with it. It's not nice for a man, it's easy for a woman, I always think. Well, somewhat easier," she amended. "Women can take things up and start again. Well, we have to, don't we, dear? We're always on a little roundabout, aren't we?"

"It's a good cake," I said.

"To think at one time I had a cook. But that was a long time ago."

Yes, a long time ago.

"You know, I saw my old cook the other day. Very nicely dressed and so on. I didn't speak. Well, you can't tell, can you? I saw old Mary, did I tell you?" she called across to Catherine. "Looking very much herself. That's one of her recipes, you're eating now," she said, returning to me. "Her good plain cake she called it. I'm glad to think she's done well. Prospered. I'd like to know how and on what."

"You could have spoken," said Catherine.

"No, better not. How did I know what she'd want? I saw my old neighbour on the bus the other day. I hadn't seen him for twelve years. Not since the morning he walked out and didn't come back. Now he's back. Working in the municipal library. Oh, that sort of thing's happening all the time now."

"Is it?"

"Oh yes. But he didn't want to speak to me. I saw at a glance. So I left it there, although he and Catherine's father had been the closest friends possible." She turned and gave her present husband a little nod and he nodded back; they seemed on perfect terms, understanding without comprehending, intimate without being close. "So he's back. Have you ever thought, my dear," she said, turning back to me and speaking in a low voice, "about what you'd do if your husband came back?"

The sweet cake clogged my mouth. I had to swallow hard.

"He died," I said, from my dry throat. "I don't think about it."

"Oh, my dear, you ought to think about it. Not dwell on it, but say to yourself 'And what would I do if he walked in tomorrow?'"

"He's dead," I repeated.

"Yes, I know. Ten years ago. But supposing he came back?"

She was right, of course, things aren't always what they seem.

"That couldn't happen to me," I said through stiff lips.

"Poor child," said Catherine's mother.

"The baby wants you to kiss her goodnight," said Catherine, coming over with her cup of coffee.

"Little love, of course I will."

"Don't let mother upset you," said Catherine in a matter of fact way. "Of course, she's right. Strange things do happen. Especially now. I feel it, don't you? The ice is breaking and people who have been caught in the ice are walking about again." She looked at me and smiled. "It could be a difficult time. So, I think we'll go to Africa."

I was wrong about Catherine; in many respects she was a very grown up girl indeed. She was looking at and observing her world. And she could take what she saw. In her way she was facing it all quite bravely.

So I got nothing out of Catherine, and if it was a farce it was one in which I was as much an object of hollow laughter as any one of the others.

There was one moment when we were open with each other. It was when I was saying goodbye to her in the narrow hall. Behind her was a mirror. I could see my own face reflected in it clearly.

I was alone now with Catherine.

"Have you been wondering why I called to see you?"

"I wasn't," she said honestly. "But my husband said you must have had some reason for coming. He felt you wanted to talk to me."

"That was clever of him."

"He is clever."

"But you didn't want to talk to me?" I knew that, because she had given me absolutely no chance to do so. Until now.

"Not really. I've got my own problems. I fight shy of anyone else's." She didn't sound like a spy talking. But motives are never easy to pin down.

"You felt sure it was a problem I was bringing here?"

"Reasonably sure, yes. We'd heard about Teddy's death. It was on the radio. Mother heard. I think that was what stirred her up. I thought there might be something you wanted help with. I didn't want to give it." She was watching the golden ball. Catherine always responded quicker and easier than the other two in submission to my questioning mind. I sometimes hardly needed to voice my queries. She also bounced back quicker.

I chanced a direct attack.

"Among my friends is someone who is prepared to betray us all and who thinks that I am still so alien that I will do the same. Is that friend you, Catherine?"

"No." She shook her head promptly. "Silly."

"Not so funny. I've got friends and I've got enemies and I'm finding it difficult to know which is which."

"Perhaps they're changing places. The untrue friend and the devoted enemy."

"You've changed your clothes since you came in, haven't you? Did you have any blood on them?"

"No." She giggled. "Only baby's dinner."

"That's a step in the right direction."

"Eh?"

"You wouldn't have stabbed a man and then gone home to feed your baby."

"Was it your friend or your enemy that did that?" Catherine said.

"I wish I knew." She was coming out of it. I prepared to close the meeting. "Goodbye, Catherine, forget I was talking."

Then it happened, the sudden reversal of our positions in which it was my mind that now lay wide open to hers. I suppose the current that ran between all of us four was so deep and strong that this was always liable to happen.

"Stella," she said, "what is it that's happening? Has he come back after all? Yes, he has. Stella, is he there with you?"

The baby wailed from its bedroom across the hall; Catherine looked at me in surprise.

"I was saying goodbye, wasn't I? I didn't mean to keep you. I'm so sorry if I've made a speech."

She kissed my cheek. Endearments were rare between us; she hardly knew what she was doing, but she meant me well.

"The baby's crying. I must go."

Then she went away and forgot to let me out and I couldn't open their door and her mother had to come and do it for me and the door stuck and it all ended on a note of farce.

My first thought was that Xandra wasn't at home, my second that it didn't matter very much. I hadn't got very much out of my expedition. Anne had talked to me and answered my questions; she had told me the truth. Catherine had reversed the process and extracted some of the truth from me. But it hadn't helped. I was no nearer knowing which of my friends had betrayed me. Even that wasn't quite an accurate way of putting it. What I ought to say was not *had* betrayed me, but was in the process of betraying me, was handing me over, bound and gagged, so that I might be a betrayer in my turn. My own fears had been skilfully used to do the binding. I was tied up in my own past and corralled by my future. I wanted to be there to have a future, I wanted to be free to enjoy it. But it was through Justine that I could be hurt. It was for her future—she hardly had a past—that I feared most.

I rang the bell twice; and was just going wearily away, when Xandra opened the door.

"Hi." This was her current affectation by way of greeting. Xandra had new little ways of speaking every time you met her. She was the one who knew the smart phrase and the 'in' word. "Well, fancy it being you." She made it sound a compliment as if she was admiring me. I wondered if she had someone with her. There had been a good pause before she let me in. Perhaps I was just getting suspicious. In my present circumstances that pause would have meant I was hiding my visitor away in the cupboard.

But her sitting room looked just as normal when I entered it. Untidy, casual and charming as usual. Like its mistress. She only had this one big room really, although there was a cupboard off it she called her kitchen and an alcove which housed the shower. I don't know where she slept, there were never any signs of her doing so, and one somehow got the impression that she perched anywhere like a bird.

Over everything tonight lay a cloud of cigarette smoke, the thick Turkish sort she liked.

"I was working," she said apologetically. She waved a hand round the room. "I need space when I work. I have to walk up and down. I can't seem to learn a line unless I'm walking." She had changed like the other two from the clothes she was wearing at lunch and now had on trousers and a silk shirt fastened with heavy gold cuff links at the wrist.

I felt my spirits rise, as always, at the sight of her. She was a life enhancer, all right. I felt that at the moment, I was definitely the opposite, a spreader of darkness rather than light.

"You do look tired," said Xandra, confirming this belief. She waved a pot. "Have some coffee."

"I've had plenty of that." Everyone seemed to think it was caffeine I needed.

"Just as well. It's cold." She tried some herself. "Well, tepid anyway." She finished the cup with apparent enjoyment. "I've got so that I don't care what heat the stuff is as long as it's *strong*."

She sat down on a long red sofa and patted the seat beside her.

"Sit down."

I cleared a space by putting a pile of photographs on a typed script. "Good play?" I asked.

"Good part, anyway," she said with a smile. "I never know what to hope for: good part, poor play, or small part but good play. Sometimes it's both, of course."

"Both good?"

"Both bad," she said with a laugh. "And then, of course, I'm bad too." She swung her legs up on to the red velvet. "Put your feet up."

I wanted her relaxed; I was glad to see her leaning back. I opened my coat so that the golden ball shone in the lamp light.

"Oh, you're wearing my present," she said idly. "Clever girl."

"Me or you?"

She laughed and closed her eyes.

"Wake up, Xandra."

When she opened her eyes they were pale and alert.

"Hear any more about Teddy?" she said. "Or Eva? It's worrying you?"

"I'm not happy about it," I admitted. "But no, I don't know any more. Not had news. I've had thoughts, though."

"Don't," she said. "Try not to think."

"That's good advice. If you can take it."

"Yes, well." She moved. "Perhaps my feet aren't as

comfortable here as I thought." She swung them down.

She'd got the room far too hot. Over in a corner of the room was a big old fashioned screen covered in embroidered silk. I wondered what would happen if I went and kicked it down and if I'd find someone sitting behind it.

I saw Xandra's eyes rest again on the golden ball.

"You know, that's a pretty thing I gave you," she said.

"I love it already." I can never be sure with Xandra. She's as likely to dominate me as the other way round. Pale eyes like hers are never easy to read, anyway. It seemed to me they were growing brighter and paler with every minute.

"I've got one myself, you know." She leaned over the back of the sofa towards the table, groped around among the objects there and pulled out an identical ball on a chain. Hers was silver, though. I made a face. "Did you think yours was the only one?"

"Put it on."

"If you like." She hung it round her neck. "Now you admire mine and I'll admire yours."

"Oh I am." But I was being careful not to look at what she was wearing; instead my gaze was unobtrusively fixed on her face. Her eyes were open, offering me a pale, admiring glance.

"Did the rehearsal go well?" I began cautiously; she had been going to a rehearsal after our meeting this afternoon.

"I was bad. I always am at first. You're lucky working with puppets."

"They can be difficult, too."

"Now I've heard everything."

"They're handled by people, after all," I said, concentrating on her, "and people make mistakes."

She didn't say a thing.

"Mistakes come expensive, don't they? I'm finding that out. In fact that's one of the things I wanted to talk to you about."

She was silent.

It was still well before midnight, but suddenly I didn't like the feel of this place or time. I was frightened.

I think Xandra felt it too. She gave herself a shake. "Don't let's talk about mistakes," she said. "Let's have a drink. I've got some whisky."

"I'm not fond of whisky." I fiddled with the chain round my neck.

"You'll like this. It's pale and empty looking but full of life." She went to a cupboard and got out a bottle filled with a golden watery looking liquid. "And stop playing with that thing you're wearing. I gave it you, remember, Stella, I gave it you."

I let her pour out the whisky and even drank a little. It was all right if you liked it.

"It's an uncivilised drink, you know," said Xandra. "All that stuff about flavour's just rot, that's not why people drink it. They'd drink it if it tasted of hay. It *does* taste of hay. Hot hay."

I drank a little more and felt bolder.

"That's right," said Xandra, watching me. "You look better now. Just now, I thought you were going to faint."

But I knew now why I had been frightened.

Sticking to my coat, which I had worn through all these three visits but not before this day, were a bunch of grey and black hairs, unmistakeably dog. I lifted my sleeve to my arm. With a shudder I thought I could almost smell dog.

I looked at the arm of the chair where I was sitting. Hairs again. Had I brought them with me, or had they been there all the time?

I sat there considering.

"Do you keep a dog?" I asked. I remembered the man who had had a photograph of a dog in his pocket.

"No."

I could have picked these hairs up at Anne's or Catherine's.

"Funny, none of us are dog lovers, are we?" I said.

"I like dogs all right. I just don't keep one."

But these hairs could have rubbed from the coat of a dog on to this chair and from the chair on to my coat.

"I thought there might have been a dog in this room."

"Why all this talk about dogs?"

"I'm allergic to dogs."

"That's new. What do they do to you?"

"They make me angry."

I got up and walked to the window. There was a small courtyard behind the house, probably the coachman and horses had lived there once, this was an old house.

"No dogs out there," said Xandra.

"Sure?" The courtyard was alternately very shadowy and brightly lit in strips. From lamps on the walls. Very confusing. In the old days, it must have upset the horses. "What do you really want from life, Xandra?" I don't know why I asked her, it just shot out. The influence of the golden ball, I expect.

"Oh, money, I suppose."

"Oh no!" I was shocked.

"Oh, other things too," she was speaking lightly. "How can I tell? Fame, achievement, one thing merges into another. Don't look so shocked. You were always the most incorruptible of us all."

She came and joined me at the window. We both saw the man, perhaps at the same minute, but only I called out. Xandra said nothing.

He was standing there looking up at where we stood. He had a bandage round his head; he couldn't have been so badly hurt as I thought. Never mind how he had got there, he was there.

CHAPTER NINE

Xandra was staring at him as if she had never seen him before in her life. I suddenly remembered how I had picked up a cushion in Anne's and hugged it to me for a moment. This could be how I had got the dog hairs in my coat.

"What's he doing here?" I said: I felt enormously practical.

"No idea. He's going away now."

"Perhaps." I watched. I wasn't at all sure he was going away. He was moving towards the entrance though and might be coming round the front of the building. "Xandra, do you remember my husband?"

"Well, of course." She sounded surprised. "We didn't meet often, I'm away such a lot, but I did come to your wedding after all."

"Would you know him if you met him again?"

"I'm not like to, am I?" she said dryly, but not, I was shocked to hear, entirely with surprise. Somehow or other she had had preparation.

"No." Not if I could help it, anyway, I thought.

"You're being a little odd, darling, you do know that?"

I didn't answer.

She moved away from the window and sat down again, taking out a cigarette. "Smoke?"

"No, thank you."

"You should always relax when you can."

"Yes, good advice." I was still at the window. "If you can take it." He was there, not moving. Perhaps he had a dog with him, perhaps not. There had to be a dog somewhere in his life.

"Have you got your answer?"

"Well, I think I have." I thought I had discovered my betrayer: Anne. Anne was in contact with the man, she knew where I was going and she had sent him round after me. Probably he had got there before me. This was how, at that moment of time, I had it worked out. It was a natural enough assumption, I suppose. "He's still there," I said.

"Is he worrying you? Shall I get the police?" She half reached out her hand for the telephone.

"No." My voice was sharp. Her hand fell away. She looked at me questioningly. "I think he may *be* a policeman." This was true enough; although I didn't like to think what branch enrolled a man such as he appeared to be. "The police aren't satisfied about Teddy's death."

"No," she said thoughtfully. "They can't be."

"I think they may be following me."

It was my belief that they certainly were following me, not because of Teddy's death, but for some other reason. One connected with the man in my flat. Nor did I think they were any orthodox branch of the police.

"It isn't quite following," she said. "It's more as if they were prowling round sniffing. Like a dog." Wondering what they could find. Yes, that was how it was.

The first thing to do seemed to be to get rid of him. I looked at Xandra. She was still sitting there, smoking and looking ready for anything. I felt that if I'd said to her, "Help me kill him," she would have agreed at once.

"Help me kill him," I said.

"Easier said than done," said Xandra, still smoking. "Got any rare drugs? Supersonic guns? Death rays? No? Got even an air pistol?"

"I could get a good sharp knife," I said.

She dismissed this as a joke, which it half was and half wasn't.

"We all could."

"I'd like to lead him a dance, though."

"How did you come here?"

"Well, I walked." Catherine, Anne, Xandra and I all lived within the same square mile, not far from the river.

"It's getting late. Time you got back."

"That's what I thought." We both stood up. Perhaps she read my thoughts or I read hers but we both knew what we were going to do.

She had a huge cupboard full of clothes, not all of them new, they must go back several years. "Just professional equipment," she said with a shrug.

"Equip me then."

"I will."

One end of the cupboard seemed reserved for a special sort of clothes. Here were the battered seedy garments which had already lived a long life. I felt I was this special sort of person at the moment.

"I call these my character parts," said Xandra. "Some of them have been invaluable to me. This coat for instance." She dragged out a black woollen coat with an attached scarf. "I wore this when I wanted to get the part of Lady Macbeth. I read the part in it. I couldn't fail. And then this," she held out a frilled cotton dress, "this was Blanche Dubois. I did all right in that too."

"Give me Lady Macbeth."

It was a big coat, Xandra was taller than me, and it nearly covered all I had on. Not quite all, enough showed somehow to make me look totally unkempt.

"Lady Macbeth of the suburbs," said Xandra, not quite in joke. "Don't murder the lodger."

She was dressing me up, putting a hat on my head and pulling my hair about my face, as if it was a game.

"This coat and hat must have a splendid strong smell of me and the theatre, not to mention the woman who owned them first—they weren't new when they came to me—so that if your follower is literally following your scent he's going to be very confused." She sounded gleeful.

She watched me go. Whether she was glad to see me go or not, I don't know.

Xandra lived on a main road; I had only a short walk towards the river, and over the bridge to get home. I had brought a follower out here with me, I didn't want to bring one back.

I walked slowly, looking back once to see if the man was following me. He wasn't there.

I shuffled along, impeded by my coat. A little hindered, too, by a confusion about what I was going back to. Whose side was I on? Was I preparing to be a traitor? Or a traitor to a traitor? What my obligations were to the man now hiding in my flat and the way of life that had put him there I was not quite clear. I appeared to have lined myself up on his side. You might say he had forced me to do so and in a sense this was certainly true, but I knew well enough there was something in me that was willing to co-operate.

I turned to look in a shop window, a battered old green-grocer's shop filled with nothing. He was behind me now.

He hadn't been deceived by my clothes. I had never really expected it.

By the laws of the society in which I lived I should wait for him and give myself up. Confess. Give up the man in my house to justice. . . . Well, we would think about justice later on.

He was moving up to me. He hadn't slowed down because I had. I wondered how it would feel if he caught up with me and put his hand on my shoulder.

I moved on from the shop and crossed the road towards the river. He too crossed the road.

But who was he? Who in fact would I be giving myself up to? What sort of man was he? Where had he come from and what did he want? Who were his allies? What was his strength? Could I afford to ignore him?

I walked along the embankment by the river.

Then suddenly I turned to face him. A clock struck midnight. Too late to run away.

He was in a dark patch just beyond a street light; when he moved forward a few feet I would see him better.

Then a bunch of laughing youngsters suddenly burst out of a side street, ran giggling and shouting to the embankment. In the middle of them was a girl with long fair hair. She seemed to be the centre of their gaiety. They were celebrating something with her. It wasn't clear what they were celebrating, perhaps nothing much, and they were certainly not rich young people, but they were alive and happy.

They formed a living barrier between me and my follower. But they were more than that: they were a reminder. They reminded me which side life was, and it wasn't on the side of the man plodding towards me. Whoever he worked for and whoever he was allied to he was on the side of death.

I turned to run across the road and down the street from which the boys and girls had emerged. I knew that at the end of it was another way home. The first street light was defective and I was running forward into darkness. My enveloping coat caught my foot and I slipped. The ground was greasy with rain and I fell hard. For a moment I was winded. Then I got up.

Behind me the man had just walked into the crowd of young people. He was walking straight through them like an automaton.

Instinctively, really without thinking, I turned and ran. The river was straight ahead, but I was not destined to get there then.

I should have got to the bridge, I think, and been across it well before the man, but the way to the bridge was blocked by a big black police car and a group of men.

I began to drag myself along like an aged woman.

My legs would hardly support me.

The young things behind me had disappeared and I didn't blame them. Who wanted to hang around?

Fear aged me with every step.

"Go ahead, mother," said one of the men by the car. He moved forward and waved me a hand. "Hurry on," he said, watching me.

I hurried. Let me give you the geography of the place. There is the bridge; by the bridge a steep flight of steps leads down to the water's edge. You can walk along the river's edge until you reach another flight of steps leading up to a street which eventually leads to another bridge. There was a rotten old warehouse on this street and it was a route more used by rats than men but eventually it would get me home.

Down the steps I half slithered and half ran.

At the bottom it had been spruced up a bit and was better than I remembered, although still a place for rats.

"Hi! Wait there!"

The shout echoed down the steps. The policeman had had second thoughts about me.

He came banging down the steps behind me, his boots making the treads ring.

Well, I could have waited, he'd asked me to, hadn't he? But somehow I didn't think I would.

But he caught up with me, he was young and eager. I could see his face.

He grabbed my arm. In resisting him, I slipped. My fall threw him off his feet and he shot forward, sliding and grabbing out, and slipping helplessly into the water.

I heard him give one shout as the current rolled him away.

It was a bad place to fall in, fierce and dirty. A terrible way to go.

CHAPTER TEN

Stephen was waiting for me when I got in. I had taken off the big coat and it was hanging over my arm. When I say waiting for me, it was after his own fashion. He wasn't to be seen when I arrived, but within a few minutes, although I did nothing except go and sit at the table and put my head on my hands, he had arrived.

He stood in the doorway between the two rooms and looked at me.

I raised my head. "Do you know that part of the river between the two bridges? Rat Walk, we used to call it. It's better now."

"I know it." Of course he did; the block of flats where Teddy had lived and he had worked was hard by. So was Anne's, for that matter.

"If someone fell in just there, would they get out again?"

"I suppose they would."

"I don't think so."

"All right, they wouldn't then." He was being deliberately calming, too calming, and it irritated me.

"Well I know who your accomplice is," I said sourly.

"Accomplice?" He didn't like the word.

"Whatever you like to call her. To me it doesn't matter, I used to call her friend."

He drew a chair up to the table and sat down beside me.

"Who is it? I too am curious."

I started to laugh. Once laughing it was not easy to stop. "Oh she's a beauty," I gasped. "Lovely to look at, clever, accomplished. A liar, too. You should meet, it's a crime you haven't. I'll arrange a meeting. Only I don't know how I'll introduce you. Shall I say: This is my husband, of course he's dead, but he's come back all the same. Or shall I say, here is an old friend of yours, but you won't remember her as you've never actually met. Or shall I say Anne, Anne, how could you?" My voice trailed away and I was crying. Silly, loose, tumbling tears that I didn't know I could cry. For years my grief had been tight and hard.

"Anne, Anne how could you?" he repeated. "The Annes always can. They're ghosts really, the Annes, that's why they don't have real feelings."

"Well, you ought to know all about ghosts," I said, shaking away my tears. "You've been one for over ten years. Tell me, what was it like down there in the underworld?"

I meant he should tell me. After all, I wanted to know what it was like if I had to join him down there.

"Not too bad." He sounded surprised that such a comment could pass his lips. "If you don't think too much about it."

"You're such a liar," I said bitterly. "I can never quite believe what you say. First you say you are my husband. I don't believe that. Then you say no, you imply you are a spy. Then you tell me you've worked for years in the block of flats where Teddy lived. I don't know if it's true. I don't remember seeing you there."

"No, perhaps none of it is true," he agreed. "Perhaps my reason for being here is quite other."

"I hate you."

"I am well aware of that."

We had reached an impasse again. It wasn't a shut door, it was one which would open if I leaned on it hard enough and it was this that terrified me. No, thank you, there are some doors it is better not to go through. Bluebeard's wife had to learn a point there.

"Now what's going to happen?"

"Nothing, I hope." He walked over and had a look

out of the window. "We shall stay quietly here. You learn down in the underworld to do that very well."

"I have been followed."

"But not by the police. Whatever they were doing by the bridge they were not looking for you. Or you would not have got away."

"Yes." I agreed with him there. "But what does the man want?"

"We don't know that he wants anything from you except perhaps to alarm you, which he seems to be doing very well."

"I connect him with Anne. And Anne is behaving oddly."

"Anne—if you are right to blame Anne—may only suspect you. She may only be looking for answers. Nor do we know how far she controls this man. She may fear him, not trust him."

But suddenly I thought I saw the answer. I was being hunted not in a human way but in the way a dog hunts.

I trembled.

"Go to bed," said Stephen. "We are safe for the moment."

"If we are safe, why don't you go away? Go home."

He was silent.

"No doubt you have a passport in one name or another. You could buy a ticket, get on a 'plane and go. Pack the whole thing up, who's to blame you?"

He was silent. Then, "It might be difficult to go back."

"You mean you'd be in trouble? They have some hold over you? You have committed some crime?"

"Only the crime of still being alive," he said with a show of feeling, for a moment, I thought, letting his real face appear. "No, I have been away a long time. Things change. I have changed. It's not my home any more."

"But neither is this city!"

He shrugged. "As much as anywhere. I carry my home on my back."

"If that is all you feel then why do you carry on? What loyalty do you owe to anything?"

"I get paid, remember," he said quietly. "Yes, that's it; I get paid."

"Go away, go away," I cried, tears falling down my cheeks. "Leave me alone."

"I can no more go away and leave you than your husband could if he was truly here," he said, with conscious self-dislike.

"Then I can see I shall have to kill you."

"Yes, perhaps." He held my arm. "But not yet."

"Why have you come here? I haven't had the real answer yet. There's still more to come, I know it."

The look on his face did not reject this.

"I have nothing to offer you," I said in a kind of wail. But I knew it wasn't true. I must have something to offer him and his masters. Even as I spoke I was searching my mind to uncover what it could be.

"I don't know," he said. That was how he said it, slowly and heavily as if he really did not know.

"Killing is the only answer."

"Yes, but you are not good at killing."

"I probably have killed one man," I said wildly. "That policeman. He wasn't so bad. He was young. Trying to do his job. I ought to have killed the other one."

"Shut up," he said, quite kindly. He went and got me a large drink out of my own store of alcohol. It didn't taste very good, but I think he had put something else in it because very soon I felt sleepy.

I staggered off, still muttering, and lay down on my bed. Just before I dropped off I struggled into wakefulness and heard myself say: "I have something to confess."

"Tell me then." He wrapped a blanket round me.

"I have two friends."

"That's not a confession; it's a hope."

"No." I was struggling for coherence. "The friend who betrayed me to you cannot be the same one as the friend that killed the man on the stairs. How could they both be on the same side?"

I didn't hear properly what he answered, but it seems to me that as I fell asleep I heard him mutter:

"Another double-headed monster in your life, you poor girl!"

The police came at the time they are always supposed to come: just before dawn would break. As I realised what was happening I remember thinking that he was wrong: we weren't as safe as all that.

I opened the door to their ring. I had to, there was no one else to do it. Perhaps I could have dragged Stephen from his hiding place, wherever that was at the moment, but leaving that aside there was only me.

I opened the door and saw them there, dark and quiet. And immediately their ringing of the bell which before had sounded huge and deafening became small and sinister. They had only made a *little* noise. That was bad. Very bad. The worst deeds happen to the accompaniment of the least noise.

I recognised them at once as the pair who had called about the death of the man in the restaurant across the road. So they were back.

I didn't speak. They didn't speak. They just walked in.

They were stern but polite, rather like the very best kind of school teacher. Or do I mean worst kind? At any rate, those with the most authority. The authority to use a stick. And what they were saying with their manner was: of course they would never use it, but the stick was there if wanted.

I've never been beaten. Once when I was little I was tormented by a tall thin boy with a length of cane. I don't remember it clearly, I suppose I have wanted to forget, but when I think about it, it seems to me we are in a wood. I don't remember where this wood was and I have never lived in the country, but in this nightmare there is a wood. I am about five. Little, anyway. But able to talk fluently like an adult. The boy on the other hand doesn't talk at all well.

"Big lazy stupid boy." I remember these words. Perhaps I brought my torment on myself by my sharp tongue.

"I'll get you." He flicks the cane across my face. He gives a sort of growl. I articulate precisely that the police will get him. There we are, the small adult-speaking figure calling on authority and the big dumb lout with a stick; it's a classic situation. I don't know how I got out of it, if I ever did. Perhaps I got beaten and bear the scars to this day.

But these men were not stupid: they were only trained to look it. I had fallen asleep wearing my top clothes and I saw them notice it.

"You've been sitting up?" one of them observed politely.

"I fell asleep."

"You weren't expecting anyone?" He was observing the room. I followed his eyes. There was no sign of Stephen's presence. To me there was unmistakable evidence of his habitation, but I hoped the policeman would not take it in. What could an opened book, a moved photograph mean to him?

"Sorry to disturb you."

"Of course." Yes, it was a lovely middle of the night for a call.

He sat down on a hard chair. His silent companion was the local boy, the one whose wife had just had a baby and whose brother drove a taxi. He didn't have much to say for himself at the best of times. He was careful not to look directly at me.

"Still, we didn't disturb you; you weren't asleep."

"Oh, I was," I corrected. "Sound asleep. You woke me up."

"In your clothes?" He looked me up and down. I

was still standing. Far away in that wood a five-year-old was screaming.

"I explained that."

"Oh, you explained?"

"I was asleep."

"Ah yes." He was silent.

"Well, it's the middle of the night."

He took a tour round the room, then he went into my bedroom. I didn't follow but from the noises he was having a good look round. Then he came out again and went into the kitchen. There, if his luck was in, he would find Stephen and he would be a made man.

But promotion wasn't coming to him that night. The telephone rang. He hurried to take the call before I could.

"Yes?"

Judging by his expression he was talking to a superior. Such a man could not show respect but anxiety sat on his face.

"Yes, yes, I'll bring her down." He turned to me. "We have a car downstairs. You must come with us."

I stared silently; I was aware that I was very close now to that five-year-old child screaming in the wood.

The morning light came through the small window set high in the wall. The light of the one electric bulb battled with the sunlight, failed and was turned out by the policeman.

I waited for him to say something. I went on waiting. I had been waiting for three hours now.

Having dealt with the electric light he went out of the room. He had been coming and going all the time. Sometimes giving me a look, sometimes ignoring me.

I shifted on the hard chair.

A tiny grey-haired old woman came in with a bucket and mop. Even police stations have to get cleaned. Still, I was surprised to see her.

She looked surprised, too. "Hello! Didn't know you was here. Thought this room was empty."

"It is, practically." I was finding speech difficult, and it was a habit I'd long fallen out of.

"You're here."

" I wish I wasn't."

"Ah well." She started to mop around. She was making the floor damp but not cleaner. That would have been difficult and she didn't look one to try for the difficult things.

"There hasn't been anyone in this room for a long while. Not like you are now. Things have been very quiet."

"Good."

"My mates and I call this the Dead End Row." She had a curious rough accent. "Well, it is at the end of the row, isn't it?" She looked to see what effect she was having.

"I don't know."

"Oh no, of course. You wouldn't know, would you?" She had another look at me. "What they got you in here for?"

"I don't know that either."

"They always say that. Nearly always, anyway. Some say they've been framed."

"You're experienced."

"I've picked up a bit one way and another." She put her head down and went on mopping.

I wondered why she was really here. To frighten me with obscure hints? She didn't have to bother. I *was* frightened.

She supplied me with a sort of answer. "Tell you what," she said. "Why don't you just go? There's no one about."

"That'd be the thing," I said ironically. "But go where?"

She looked thoughtful. Perhaps she was going to offer me her bucket and mop and her old boots and let me plod out pretending to be her.

"If you knew this place like I do, you'd know there're times you could walk out and no one'd know." She gave her hoarse laugh again. "They're not so efficient."

I could see that her tiny little battered boots were several sizes too small for her and immensely uncomfortable.

Suddenly this made me certain she was quite genuine. Mad but genuine.

"You'll soon know what it's all about," she said without warning. "That is, if you're ever going to know. Here comes the Inspector."

She must have had sharp ears, but sure enough, she was right and in a moment he came hurrying into the room, black brows drawn. He wasn't pleased to see the cleaner.

"What are you doing here? You shouldn't be here."

"I'm sorry. Just going."

"You talk too much." He held open the door. "Clear off."

"Someone has to clean. I know my job. And my rights."

"You're lucky then."

He didn't sound nearly so unpleasant as I'd thought and he turned to me when she'd gone, quite politely.

"I'm sorry we had to bring you down here in the middle of the night and then leave you waiting. But to tell you the truth we had a period of intense anxiety."

I nodded.

"Oh yes." He didn't add any details but sat down facing me. Apparently I wasn't to go home yet. "A cigarette?"

"No, thank you."

"You'd like something to drink? Yes, of course." He went to the door and called to someone in the corridor. As far as I remembered this corridor, which led straight from the front door of the police building, had six doors in it. I was behind the sixth and last. There were big black double doors at the end. Dead End, as my friend the cleaner had accurately observed.

He sat down then and waited without saying anything.

Very soon a tray came along with two thick white cups on it, one for him and one for me. It looked like coffee, and it smelt like coffee. It didn't taste like it, though.

He drank his thirstily, watching me over the top of his cup.

"Not good?" he said. "It seems all right to me. I don't taste it. To tell you the truth I don't taste anything. I have lost my sense of smell." He touched his long crooked nose gently. "An accident. And when the smell goes, taste goes with it. No, it's some years since I have tasted anything." Once again he touched his nose reminiscently; I fancied it might have been broken once. "It's a drawback, of course. But you learn to live with it, you learn to live with it."

"Well, about what was worrying us." He smiled, showing a gap in his teeth, perhaps they'd gone when the nose got its injury.

"I'd like to know why you've got me here."

"I asked you to come and you came," he reproved, although I didn't remember exactly being asked. "But yes, I can see you want to know what the problem was. And if I tell you as much as I can, then in return you must tell me what you know."

"If I know anything."

"Oh, you'll know something. Yes, I think you'll find you know something. I hope so." Black brows, broken nose, gap in teeth. What a beauty. But trying hard to be polite.

I put my cup on the table, just balancing it on the edge. "I'll have that cigarette now," I said. It was my first, very faint touch of aggression towards him.

It was a mistake. He gave way to the instant desire to knock me back.

"*Now* I don't have one," he said.

I lowered my eyes. It was better really not to show anger.

"Just have a look at this," he said, putting a photograph on the table in front of me. "Have you seen him? Do you know him?"

"No. I told you that before." It was the photograph, now much enlarged, of the man who had died in the café across the road from where I lived. The man who, according to Elizabeth, had been looking up at my windows. "Perhaps I may have seen him when he was alive. But now he's dead. People look different. I don't recognise him."

I remember I closed my eyes at this point, as if shutting out the memory of what I had seen. In a way, what I had said was true enough; I felt as though I had never seen that face in life. Yet the features held something familiar to me.

"He looks to me a person you'd easily recognise," he said, squinting at the photograph of the dead face. "Strong features. You'd remember that face, I should say. Good photograph, too."

"Yes." I might as well give him an agreement where I could.

"He was a man called Ernest Braun, or Brun. He seems to have spelt it in several different ways. It's not a very good name, is it?"

"Not very," I said, wondering what he meant.

"By which I mean it can't have been his real name."

"It must be *somebody's* real name," I said.

"Oh yes, but not his. He borrowed it as a matter of fact, from a real Ernest Braun who died in 1945. Who *probably* died then. Naturally we don't know precisely. One Braun went out and another came in. And you're sure you don't know him?"

I shook my head.

"He lived, in an unobtrusive way, just around the corner from your brother-in-law. They knew each other. You understand what I'm telling you?"

I understood. Ernest Braun was a threat to the state, a menace to security (everyone's, his own included).

"I don't believe Teddy did anything wrong in his whole life," I said carefully. "He was too ambitious."

"He was an important man," he agreed.

"If he killed himself it was because he was afraid, not because he was guilty."

Two other people had moved into the room with us, Teddy and his wife Eva. They weren't entirely voluntary guests: they had been summoned up by us two. I wondered if Eva in the flesh was here with us in this building or if she had been taken elsewhere. Wherever she was I don't suppose she was wearing her shiny fur coat.

"You said Teddy knew this man. Very well. You must know what you are talking about. But if he did, only innocently, not as a spy."

"His wife Eva thinks differently."

"Poor Eva."

"Don't waste pity on her." He sounded grim. "She is a guilty woman. You always got on well with her?"

I thought for a moment. "Yes."

"Never had a quarrel?"

"No."

"No reason to think her a liar?"

I wondered which way he was going. "Not more than most women of her type," I said.

That little touch of aggression again. The cup wobbled on the edge of the table and crashed to the floor. More aggression, kinetic force emanating from me. He responded to it at once.

"You wouldn't call her an enemy of yours?"

"She might be."

"Look at this photograph again. Here." He pushed the dead man's face at me again.

I pushed it away. "No need, I don't know him."

"Your sister-in-law says he was her husband's brother. *Your* husband."

I looked at the floor. The cup and saucer, broken in their fall, still lay there. I studied it very carefully. Finally I said: "She *is* a liar then." My anger gathered force. "Mad, too. She knows my husband is dead. Ten years. Ten years he has been dead." My voice was rising.

"Yes, I've heard that. You live as a widow."

"I live the way I am."

"What about your husband, eh? Seen him lately?"

"Shut up about my husband," I exploded. "He's dead. Gone. I've got over it. I never even think of him."

He accepted this. I'm not saying he didn't know I was lying, he probably did. But for him a lie was as good as the truth: he knew the area I was sensitive in now.

All the time we had been talking his long dry fingers had been keeping up a little dance on the edge of the table.

While Teddy had been alive, he had, by virtue of his position and the power he had gathered, somehow protected us all. Perhaps we hadn't liked him too much but he was an important person and his name meant something. Now he was gone. Worse, he had died in such a way that a question mark now hung about him.

"Still, it's a strange lie," he said. "I think she believed it."

"Don't let's make a serial out of it," I said.

"Naturally it alarmed us. Security-wise, as the Americans say." He attempted a charming smile. "It threw a spanner in the works."

"It isn't true."

"She knew something about him, more than you think perhaps. Oh yes."

"My sister-in-law's contact with my late husband was minimal. And whatever she and Teddy had been doing I had nothing to do with it. I don't know any state secrets, I have no access to any. I am totally uninteresting."

"Oh, you have a contact all right."

"Who?"

"What? You don't know?" He gave me a look that

implied I couldn't be that innocent.

He got up and went to the door. He listened. There was no noise, not even the noises you might expect in a building of this sort. Then he came back.

"Thought we might be disturbed."

He had left the door open, wide open, I could see right through to the corridor. I didn't think this was by chance.

Then I did hear something. First a voice saying a phrase I couldn't quite hear, but it could have been "Hurry up". Then footsteps. But not clear crisp sounds like people really walking along to a destination they wanted to go to, but slurred sounds. I made out that it was more than one person.

I turned my eyes away and fixed them on the floor where I studied the broken cup. In my mind was the thought that if I counted up to a hundred this would give the procession time to get past.

I couldn't close my ears, though. Without flinching they picked up heavy breathing and those unnerving slow feet.

Then there was a sort of sucking sound, an unbearable noise. I had to look up.

There they were going past; Eva and her gaolers. I was in time to see her walk past between them. She was walking very very slowly, they on either side of her as if guiding her, and staring straight ahead of her. She looked like a woman frightened into silence. As she walked she took deep breaths through her half-opened mouth and it was this action that made the strange noise I had heard. I suppose it was quite involuntary.

I got up and stood rigidly as she walked past. She didn't turn her head to look in the room; I doubt if she saw the door or would have seen me if she'd looked. She wasn't seeing anything in this world at all.

"Eva!" I cried.

"She doesn't see you," he said. "Doesn't see anything perhaps. Well, shock, you know."

"What has happened to her?"

"Well, she's confessed."

"Confessed?"

"She killed the agent in the restaurant. Poison. Your husband or not your husband, whichever he was. She knew how to go about it," he laughed. "You can't beat these countrywomen."

"How did she do it?"

"She gave him a minute cyanide-gelatine capsule slipped into a drink. He just swallowed it down. Perhaps he'd asked her for a headache cure. Who knows?" He laughed at his joke. "The effect was delayed until the gelatine dissolved in the stomach. Perhaps she wishes she'd taken one herself now. We found she had one."

"Eva was in the Restaurant Elizabeth?"

"The Yugoslav proprietress can identify her."

"I see." So that was why Elizabeth had been so interested and watchful with me. She knew Eva was my sister-in-law. She must have been wondering how much I knew about it all.

"Why did she do it?"

"He was her contact with us. She was wiping out someone who threatened her. Events were beginning to catch up with her as they usually do with ladies like her. She knew what she had to look forward to."

"She looked terrible."

"You ought not to mind. Cleared you, didn't it? Once she'd said that, I almost apologised for getting you down here. I will apologise if you like."

He looked as bold and unpleasant as before.

He got up and bowed me to the door. I had played my part in his black comedy. I wasn't sure how much he still suspected me nor of what. And I suppose that was what he intended.

He offered me a ride home in an official car, which was kind of him, but I refused.

So he let me out into the morning.

CHAPTER ELEVEN

I emerged into a sombre side street. It was a dry quiet morning. What a pity *he* had to be there, the man. But he was there, and I knew he had to be. I wanted to feel surprise, I tried to summon it up, but it wouldn't come. I had no surprise.

He was standing across the road, back to a brick wall, looking, perpetually looking. It was the clearest I had seen him so far. He was small, dark skinned with greying cropped hair. I could see a patch of grubby plaster on his head where I had wounded him. He had anonymous features and on his feet were dry powdery shoes as if he walked a good deal.

I made an exclamation which the young policeman at the gate heard.

"Who is he?"

"I've seen him before," admitted the policeman.

"Is he a beggar?"

"Beg?" he said contemptuously. "What is there to beg in this city? No."

"Just a workman," I said thoughtfully.

"She paints a pretty picture," said the blue-suited investigator. "She tells her story well. Did you really look like that?"

"It was a part I had established for myself."

His interrogator stared bleakly at him. "You seem to have been more noticeable than you imagined."

"Oh, it's all right for you. You were sitting here. I was out there in a hostile city. Two of us were dead. My contacts were working class. I had to stay near them.

"And what's all this about a dog?"

"My landlady's. It belonged to the woman where I stayed."

I waited. It was no time to stand still but I found myself unable to move. Sweat moved on my face. Fatigue and fear did something odd to time. The minutes seemed to run on and on. He was crossing the road, he was still crossing the road, he was still crossing it.

During this time I had plenty of chance to wonder what he was. But I couldn't make up my mind. Not what he seemed: that was certain.

He moved towards me. I think he was going to speak. I felt at once that he was rapacious, a hungry, seeking mind.

Once he got a word out, whatever the language, I was done for. I turned and ran.

As I ran I thought I heard a call.

"So you never spoke to her?" said the questioning voice.

"Not face to face. Not then," came the answer. "But later, of course, I caught up with her. Indeed at that point, when she ran away, I was quite happy with the way things were turning out. I was setting up the conditions which would make our meeting a success when it did take place. A success on *my* terms."

I wasn't sure what I was running from now or why. Everyone knew where I was. They even knew what they wanted from me. Only I didn't know.

Even now at home, Stephen was waiting for me. He hadn't told me what he wanted to chip out of my life, but he knew all right.

"I know what I'll do," I thought. It was mad. "I'll have a perm."

Sometimes, on a Sunday, Antoinette could be persuaded to redo and refurbish my hair. It wasn't quite

a permanent wave but a method she had invented.
She had to be coaxed, though.

I felt today I could coax her. I felt I could have
coaxed a lioness into giving up her young one's dinner.
I *was* a lion's dinner.

Plenty of people were wanting to take great bites at
me. It made me drunk. I was intoxicated with the
hunt; perhaps this was how the fox felt as it ran.

I trotted up the stairs. Antoinette was just poking
her head round her front door to see if her newspaper
had arrived. She only took one on Sunday and was
always anxious to get it.

"Where have you been?" she said; she always took
a slightly parental attitude to me.

"Just walking."

"What, all night?"

"No, of course not. Early morning."

She looked sceptical. "My dear, your face. Haggard
isn't the word. You haven't been drinking, have you?"

"No."

"Well, you're a mystery." She prepared to close her
door.

"Antoinette, do my hair this morning."

"Well . . ."

"Please."

"I'm a working woman, you know." But she was
weakening.

"Oh, go on."

"Well . . ." She put her head on one side. "There's
a lovely new way on big rollers I could try."

"Later this morning?"

She nodded. "About eleven. Won't take me long.
Mind you, allow me proper time. Not one of your
wild rushes. I'm not one of these quick and hasty
workers. I'm an artist."

"I'll be there."

Perhaps it sounds mad, crazy; to come back from
the police and have my hair done. But it wasn't really.
I was merely signalling I meant to survive. To have my

hair set showed I was going to live. I wasn't going to be one of those who went under.

I let myself quietly into my flat. I wasn't going to call out or act as if anyone was there. How did I know who *was* there?

He said it for me, though. "Is anyone there?" he called, standing in the kitchen door.

"You knew it was me." I threw my coat on a chair. It narrowly missed Atabi, who rose up with dignity and moved off. "Or you wouldn't have called out."

He didn't say he was glad to see me back; he didn't have to. His safety and mine were indivisible. Except, of course, he wasn't thinking only of safety; he was here with a purpose.

I looked at him standing there, still, composed, determined. And so was I. He wanted to use me, was already doing so. I was beginning to guess in what manner. But I was going to make use of him. There was plenty to learn on both sides.

"What happened?"

Oh, so he was curious. "Not too much really. More may be going to happen, of course. I don't know. They are worried about Teddy primarily and Eva. Not you. They don't appear to know about you. Oh, they must suspect there's someone like you in the background, but about you as you they seem to know nothing. No, you are safe."

"I wasn't worried about that."

"Oh, indirectly you must be." I allowed a little touch of the lash to creep in. I wasn't contemptuous of him, but I was up against him now, face to face, and we would have to fight it out. "You've come here on business, you want to live to complete that."

"I don't suppose anyone is going to kill me."

"Oh, I think they might do." I laughed. "I suppose just that." Atabi called out nervously from his seat by the window. He didn't like the mood I was in; he was a good judge of a situation. "I've been out in the world, remember, while you've been sitting here and

I've seen what's going on. Whether the police are looking for you or not, I don't really know, but they must be looking for the person you are and they may find you. Probably they won't kill you, but they may; they seem to be clumsy men. But we have another enemy, you and I."

For the first time I coupled us. He didn't like it.

"You're talking wildly," said Stephen in a cold voice.

"No, not wildly. I'm confused; it's a confusing situation. I don't really know what's happening. But I'm not wild. I feel quite cold inside."

Silently he went out and returned with a tray on which a breakfast, coffee and toast, was neatly arranged. He had used my best china. This annoyed me.

He poured coffee for us both.

"You had it ready," I said.

"I had it ready. I knew you'd be back."

"I will describe this man to you. Fortyish, short greying hair, cropped short. I don't remember his features; I haven't seen him close or in a good light."

"Did you see him from the back?" he asked after a pause.

"No."

"You might try," he suggested.

"I hope I never see him again. He's a man of regular habits. Turns up at the same time at the same place. Rather odd times and places. Do you know him?"

"He sounds an ambiguous character."

"He's worse than that," I said with conviction. "He's a sort of businessman, only he's after destruction."

"A good diagnosis," he said sombrely. "It fits too many people, though."

"She was a friend of mine," I said, draining my coffee. "Anne, I mean. Yet she betrayed me. She is conspiring with this man."

"Now you are going wild again."

"She's a traitor and a liar. So are you. A liar anyway." I was terribly tired.

"I haven't told you so many lies."

"You're all one big lie." I was utterly exhausted, but burning inside with a fierce energy.

"Now you've covered it all!"

"Well, they let me come away. They don't really suspect me of anything. They know nothing of you. Nothing of Anne. You are in league with Anne, she is in contact with the man who follows me. Therefore he must want to get in touch with you or me. But for what purpose? It's very confusing." Ideas were circling in my mind, they seemed to catch each other's tail, and then change into something else. No one had any true identity. Everyone was in a perpetual state of metamorphosis, except the dead.

"Justine telephoned," he said.

"You spoke to her?"

"I had to. A sweet voice. She is anxious about you. She is also anxious about the old mother of Eva she has staying with her."

"I bet she is." I remembered the old mother. She had a temper like a saw and a tongue to match it.

"Justine will telephone again."

"I don't want her to."

"She will even be coming round."

"I suppose you arranged that. I've been wondering when you would."

He ignored this. As he could afford to. I wondered why I had ever felt a softness towards him. Then he put his hand on my shoulder and I knew.

"You are trading on your name," I said sullenly. "Stephen. One of my husband's names was Stephen."

"You're still young. You could marry again."

"I want things, not people."

"No, that's not true. It makes you sound hard: you are above all a person who is not hard. You value people."

"And look where it's got me," I said bitterly.

"And look where it's got me." He said it awkwardly, reluctantly.

I looked him long in the face, then I turned away. "No. I don't believe it."

"You believe it because it's the same for you too."

"Never."

"Yes, I'll accept never," he said, after thinking about it. "The odds are against anything ever coming of it, but that's not the same as no."

"Don't mistake me; I'm hostile."

"I'm not making a mistake."

I was grudging, unwilling to give ground. "Just having you here has made me remember things. It's nothing more than that."

"And when I've gone?"

"If you ever go," I put in.

"Will memories be enough then?"

I didn't answer.

"You know they won't be. You're alive. Perhaps you were dead for a little while. But not any longer."

I muttered something, I hardly knew what I was saying, but even my ears caught only the word painful.

But he caught it, he had sharp hearing. "Yes, we have both been dead and know that it is painful to come alive again. The blood runs, the muscles ache again, the nerves are sharp."

He was too articulate by half.

"I have some grey hairs, do you know that?" I said.

"Not really grey, are they? Just a little powdering. Pretty." He added, with that touch of candour I had come to expect from him: "Anyway you have a very good way of doing your hair so that you cover it up."

"I'm having it done again this morning. Antoinette is doing it for me."

"Don't let her spoil it."

"If you said that in a voice one shade less astringent, it would be tender."

"Don't let her spoil it."

This time the silence was bitter-sweet.

"You're a liar and I'm a fool," I said sadly.

Then perhaps we may have kissed. Isn't it strange I

don't remember? Or perhaps it would be stranger if I could. Some moments are born to disappear. We are consumed by them.

I remember standing in the window, looking down at the street and stroking Atabi. I felt shy and a little awkward.

There was nothing sure, nothing positive about the way I felt then. I was hesitating. Not love, not yet. It was still a step away. Heard but unbelievable. Like a master playing a violin in another room.

My doorbell rang. I knew who it was at once. Justine.

"I wish she hadn't come," I said. "I'll open it. You needn't hide."

I walked to the door and flung it open. I had been very quick. Stephen had had no time to move. I suppose you could say I really wanted to show him to the world. There stood Xandra.

"Hello." Her eyes found Stephen at once, but she showed no surprise; she had a natural poker face when it suited her. "I expect you're surprised to see me so early."

"I'm surprised to see you."

"Goodness, you look tired." She had put on a pair of the huge spectacles she had affected lately and was studying my face. "I've got so short-sighted this last year." Perhaps she really hadn't seen Stephen. But she had, though, and gave him a radiant smile. I introduced him, calling him Mr. Green. I knew as soon as I'd done it that I needn't have bothered. For some reason she didn't care whether she knew his name or not. Probably she had her own ideas about why he was there. But behind her big spectacles it wasn't easy to read her expression. She shook Stephen's hand politely and when he dropped his cigarettes she picked them up. It wasn't like Xandra to be so polite.

"The thing is I've got to go away."

"Oh, another play? Another production?"

"Yes, that's it. Another production."

"Are you going straight away?"

"Not at once. I've got to finish up here first. But quite soon."

"Bring me back a present."

"Oh I will. What would you like?"

I laughed without answering. Xandra's presents were unpredictable. Her travels somewhat resembled a war campaign and the things she brought back with her were war-loot. You took what you got.

"I see you're still wearing my golden ball," she said.

"Yes." I tossed it between my hands.

"You know it opens?"

I shook my head.

"Yes." She came over. "Here's this little knob and you pull it. There's nothing inside, of course. I left that for you to do. A bit of cotton wool with scent in it, that sort of thing. That's what it's meant for." She had pulled the golden knob and the ball fell into two halves and was indeed quite empty. "Yes, that's it," she said, snapping it shut.

"Are you going round saying goodbye to all your friends?"

"Well, hardly." She laughed, one of her lovely golden phoney laughs.

As I saw her out I said: "You didn't really come just to say goodbye."

"No."

She stood still for a moment.

"I am going away, of course." She frowned. "Really good offer. One I couldn't turn down. I wanted to see you. You seemed in an odd state yesterday."

"Not really."

"I thought so. But that isn't why I came. You're about the most honourable person I know. I want you to keep something for me."

"Here?" I was thinking of a piece of furniture, an animal.

"Yes. It's not big." She produced a white envelope

about six inches long from her handbag. It was sealed. "Can you?"

I looked at it. "Is it something personal?"

"Yes, in a way." She looked at me and smiled. "It's all right. It won't explode. I don't want to take it out of the country. And I'd like to think it was in your hands."

I still hesitated.

"I doubt if it's very safe here, Xandra," I said at last.

"Nonsense. What could happen here? Keep it."

"Can I know what it is?"

"You can know when you hand it back to me." She gave me her brilliant smile.

"I will be giving it back to you?" I asked slowly.

"Goodness yes. I'm not going to die."

"I don't understand you," I said.

"Nor I you. But we've been friends a long while. Keep it for me." She put it into my hands. I took it.

"Anne's mad," she said, in a conversational way. "Or she's close to those who work in madness."

I stared, remembering little incidents about Anne's youth. How once she had worked thirty-six hours non-stop without sleep and almost without food because she said she 'must'. How she had suddenly stopped talking to her own sister because of a difference of opinion.

"Nothing counts with her now, no human ties," said Xandra urgently. "No love, friendship or loyalties. She's inhuman. She would sacrifice anything."

"What a group we turned out to be," I said. "And what about you? Are you the same?"

"You know I'm not. Nor are you."

"It's funny how much everyone seems to know," I said, "more about me than I know myself. Goodbye, Xandra."

"Goodbye." She looked at me for a moment and then went running down the stairs.

When I came back into the room Stephen was shaving. Or rather, preparing to do so.

He had put his electric razor, plugged in and oper-ating, down on a chair and it was whirring away on its own, its teeth quietly chewing away at nothing. To my strung up imagination there was something sinister and menacing about its activity.

"I didn't know you had an electric razor," I said.

"Yes, I assumed you searched my things. I do have one though. You missed it."

"The other old safety one was really my husband's, wasn't it?" I sat down and looked at him.

"Yes. It was meant to convince you."

"You did know my husband then? He is really dead?"

"Yes," he said, after a pause. "He's dead all right."

"That's something solid under my feet then."

"No, it's not. Never mind why it's not solid, but it's not."

"You're not using the razor to shave," I said.

"No." He picked it up. "It has other uses." He felt it, apparently it wasn't ready for him yet, so he put it back on the chair. "And what did she really want?"

"Xandra? Your guess is as good as mine. A look at you perhaps."

"She knows about me?"

"She's not supposed to."

Now his instrument was ready for him. He picked up the razor with its steel jaws still working. But these didn't interest him. It seemed to be the temperature that he was concerned with.

"I didn't know razors got hot."

"This one does." He smiled at me, the sort of smile that no one wants. We were no longer reacting to each other. Xandra's arrival had stopped all that. Business was on again.

From nowhere a piece of paper appeared on the table. It was about nine inches by six. I was surprised he let me see it, but I suppose he no longer cared.

"Instructions?" I said.

"Could be." He got on with the job. He applied the

surface of the razor, now nicely hotted up, to the
paper. A string of writing appeared.

"So that's what the razor is for."

"Yes. It provides exactly the right degree of heat."

The string of writing was spreading out across the
page, covering nearly all of it.

"I can see it quite clearly from here," I pointed out
to him.

"It wouldn't mean much to you." Yes, he must be
quite sure of me, confident I couldn't hit back.

He read down the page, then reread it. At no point
did his expression change. I watched him anxiously
wondering what he was reading. My life as well as his
was going to be altered by that writing which had
come out of nowhere to stand clear and bold on the
page. Did he understand how much his future was
under fire too? He looked calm; he thought he had
nothing more to lose. I wondered if he knew how
much he still had to lose. There is always that little bit
more than you knew.

And there is always someone around to see you lose
it.

"Why are you doing this now?" I asked suddenly.

He ignored it for a moment and then said, "It's the
time for it."

"But why *now*?"

"Let's leave it at that."

Nothing moved his calm. But someone was going to
have to throw a bomb at him quite soon and that
someone was probably me. I wondered where George
was. I hadn't seen him for some time now.

After he'd read the letter three times he rose.

"Now you're going to burn it, I suppose," I said.

He gave me a dry smile; after all, he hadn't very
much liked what he'd read. "No. In certain circumstances ashes can be recovered and read."

He went out to the kitchen and came back with a
small bowl of water which he set on the table. Then
he put the piece of paper in the bowl. For a moment

it floated on the surface. Then before my eyes it turned slowly into a transparent jelly, crumbled into pieces and gradually disappeared.

"Cellular paper," he said, watching my gaze.

"It was kind of you to let me see that exhibition."

"I don't want you, or anyone, looking for a paper that isn't there. Remember. It no longer exists."

"You exist, though," I said cruelly; he didn't know I could be cruel. "And someone could make you tell."

He smiled. Another one of those smiles that is a close relation to a sting. "Pain won't do it." He looked at his wrists. If those scars were his prize, he had cause to feel triumphant. Prize or proof, sometimes there is no difference.

"Perhaps pleasure would?"

"It might come nearer. But the answer must be no. Don't let me deceive you."

"You don't deceive me nearly as much as you think. Not nearly as much."

We eyed each other. God knows who was the greater liar.

"I do admire you," he said slowly. "I really do. The way you've behaved in this situation. The way you've kept your head. The way you've fought on, kept on trying to make things go your way. You're still trying, aren't you?"

It was my turn now to keep silent and offer him that antismile.

"Why don't you go down and get your hair done?" he said in a level voice.

"Justine's coming in."

"Not just yet." He sounded quite sure.

Just then the telephone rang and it was Antoinette. "You coming down?" she said. "I'm all ready, I can't wait for ever."

I went down, still in the odd determined mood as if this was one thing I had to get done.

Antoinette was bustling around, playing her usual game of pretending to be the temperamental artist who couldn't work unless conditions are just right. "Now where's the mirror? I've got to have my black comb, it's my other hand, that comb. Hurry up, girl, you know I have to do this while I have the inspiration." No one was less temperamental than Antoinette really, she was as solid as a rock. Basalt, that veined, dark-coloured, ex-volcanic rock, for preference. And yet one often got the feeling with Antoinette that the volcano was only recently defunct.

She started combing me out. "Let's get on with it."

She had my hair right over my face. "Mm-m," I muttered.

"You're not so talkative." She pushed my head down into the shampoo. "This is something special I'm using on you. You're the first person who's used it. Well, the second person, the first wasn't really fair. She didn't tell me her hair was dyed. How's it feel?" She didn't wait for me to answer. "I'm going to set it on special big rollers."

"If anything happens to me," I said, "will you look after Atabi?"

"Why should anything happen to you?"

"I don't know. Like you, I feel uneasy."

"If anything did happen to you, as you put it, you know very well that Atabi would make his own demands to me. I've been his second home for years."

"He loves no one really."

"That's the way to be," said Antoinette cheerfully.

I looked at my face in the mirror. She was quite right, my hair looked soft and pretty. "You are clever," I said.

"I've got another new thing I'd like to try another time," she said. "You've got the hair for it. More of a wave. A little more tint at the temples, too." She stood back to admire her creation.

"I'd like that," I said. "I will if I can." It was something to look forward to.

"That George," she said, as if she had been saving

up her news for last. "I always said he'd be in trouble."

"What's happened?"

"The police found him and a gang of friends hiding out in some cemetery, playing at mock funerals." She clicked her tongue.

"It doesn't sound bad trouble." But I was alarmed.

"The police have packed it up, anyway," said Antoinette with some satisfaction. "I don't think it was nice, what they were doing." She made her eyes round with hints of necrophilic horrors. "Anyway, it's all packed up," she repeated.

"I see." So there was another promising little empire gone.

"And they're sending George away. So they say."

"Who says?"

"The couple who look after him."

"I must try and see him before he goes," I said. I was disturbed and unhappy at the news.

"If you can."

"What do you mean?"

She shrugged. "He's not the sort to hang about, is he? Do you think he'll stay to have the police put him away? I haven't seen him around today."

I was deeply worried about George. I looked around me, wondering if George would spring out from a corner. But he wasn't there.

I let myself in quietly. Justine was there. Sitting on a low chair with her long legs stretched in front of her and smoking.

"Alone?" I said, looking round.

"Not really." She smiled. Her eyes rested on the kitchen door. "I've been made welcome."

I bet, I thought. That's the welcome the tiger gives to the goat.

"He's an enigma, though, isn't he?" She smoked a little, then said, "Do I call him father?"

"I don't know." I was hesitant. "Do you?"

"No. On the whole, I think not." She got up and

started to move about the room; she was more under pressure than she wanted to show. "That's entirely without prejudice. I haven't made up my mind."

I helped myself to one of her cigarettes. It was bitter and rather horrible; I wondered if she'd made them herself. She grew tobacco one year round my little hut in the country that we used at weekends. This summer, if I lived long enough, we were going to build in brick. I thought about the bricks.

"What's the matter with you? You look odd."

"It's my hair."

"No, not entirely. Where is he now? Does he always disappear like this?"

"Yes. It's one of the things about him." Come to think of it, it was built into his history. Whether he was this man or that one, he must always have been a good disappearer.

When he appeared at the kitchen door, Justine was watching him and I was watching her.

"I don't remember you," she said sadly.

"Don't try to."

"It was better when we were talking on the telephone. Then I kept getting the feeling that, yes, I did know your voice, that there was something I remembered. It's all gone now."

"Let's leave it at that." He sat down at the table.

"Yes, do," I said. "Leave it, leave it, leave it."

Justine looked at me in surprise. "Oh, I can't do that."

"I don't want you to," said Stephen. "Would I be here if I did?"

"No, I don't suppose so." She considered him. "Why are you here?"

"Don't ask him, please don't ask him, Justine."

"Why not?"

"He might tell you. He's had his orders."

"Of course, he's going to tell me." She was very calm. "I am here for him to tell me."

"No, Justine, that's dangerous."

"Yes, it is dangerous. Everything has been dangerous since he came here."

"Since just before," corrected Stephen in a mild voice. "Since the time when your researches achieved a certain success."

"Not just my researches. Other people have worked with me."

"Oh certainly, but let's not take your medal away. Most of the work was yours. You're getting a medal, by the way, did you know that? Congratulations."

"I did know," said Justine.

"As soon as you got to a certain point in your work (which is very important isn't it?), you became important yourself."

"So now I know why you came."

"I'm not entirely sure if I know myself," he said ironically. "I only know what I have been instructed to do. The actual information to be extracted from you will be someone else's work. I am no scientist."

"You know it's a scientific discovery," I said.

"It didn't take much telling, did it?" Not once did he look my way. He was cold and assured. "A great scientific discovery, I believe."

"But these things are published," I cried. "The whole world will know."

They were both dead silent. I could see that they were quietly agreed on one point: if this great scientific discovery could be kept as one nation's secret then it would be.

"Anything can happen in this country," said Stephen. "Be reasonable. You know that. No. I don't foresee Justine making a world publication of her work just yet."

"*Our* work," she corrected coldly.

"We mean to have it, Justine."

"Justine," I said urgently, "get up from that chair and get out of this room. At once."

She didn't move.

"Yes, why don't you, Justine?" asked Stephen. I

hadn't helped Justine, I had merely strengthened him.

"Do you think I haven't been approached before?" asked Justine contemptuously. "Are you the first to get on to me? There's more than one way of doing it, you know. Some people do it with a smile and not a threat. You're less subtle. Why don't you try money?"

"Well, we have," he said with a smile. "In one of my other manifestations, I tried money. You turned it down."

"Perhaps you didn't offer enough."

"I will bargain if you like," he said slowly.

"No."

"I haven't really offered you threats."

"It's written all over you," she said, running her eyes up and down him.

"I'll kill him if he hurts you, Justine," I cried, my voice shaking. They ignored me. I wasn't there.

"I'm trusted, you know," said Justine to him. "I've been investigated and proved clean and I'm trusted. Even when Teddy and Teddy's wife turned out to have been in a big mess I haven't been in any trouble."

"I have," I said bitterly.

"Yes, Stella, I know. I'm sorry." Now she did look at me. Then back again to him. "So I am trusted, but I am *also* watched. Routine. But still, it is done."

"But I'm well placed here, aren't I? No one knows I'm here. And there's no reason why you shouldn't visit your stepmother."

"The answer's still no."

"Think about it."

"I won't change my mind; I've had plenty of time to think about it. I told you I've been approached before."

"But this is the first time by someone inside."

"You wouldn't use Stella," she cried.

"I might have to."

So then I knew how it was and how all along I had been deceived. I had thought that Justine was to be used to bring pressure on me, now I saw that it was the other way round—my position was quite other, and I was to be the threat held over Justine's head.

My beautiful lovely Justine whom I wanted so much to protect. All this charade of husband reappearing, father coming back, was really aimed at her. Because I had secret political affiliations in my past I could be used against her.

There were three protagonists in the room. Two of them held each other in check. Very well, I thought, that leaves it up to me.

We have got richer, we own more things, there is even hope in the air, but we haven't got any better. The other way round perhaps. Every year there is a harder fall, a different breed of men.

"Go into the kitchen and make us some coffee," said Stephen, turning to me.

"Yes, do go, Stella," said Justine, never taking her eyes from his face. "Leave us alone just a little while to talk."

"I'd rather be here."

"We have to talk."

I went into the kitchen. I made coffee. It was a bitter brew. I laid out cups on a tray and carried it through to them. They were seated at opposite sides of the table and I wasn't sure that they had come to any agreement.

Stephen took his cup and stirred in some sugar. He looked as composed as usual. Justine was flushed, a blotch of colour on her neck.

She drank the coffee and rose to go. Oddly enough, she shook Stephen's hand. I thought it meant something.

She had a last word for him at the door. "Your own position is not so good, I suppose you know that? Once your job here is done, who is going to look after you? You are expendable."

Yes, he knows that. He says nothing, but I see it on his face.

Then she is gone and has left him to me. I closed the door. I locked it. I think this struck him as remarkable, even sinister, but he knew better than to speak.

"Now we are shut in alone together," I said. It was a promising beginning.

"Don't do anything silly," he said.

"That means don't do anything violent, don't do anything that cuts across what I want, don't do anything without telling me."

"That about covers it."

I smiled.

"You're harder than I realised," he said, giving me a close look.

Oh, and much harder still, I thought.

"You haven't finished your coffee," I reminded him.

"Very strong," he said, picking it up and draining it down. "Probably induce insomnia."

"No, it won't do that."

"It is a little early in the day to sleep," he admitted. We might have been an ordinary married couple, talking over the coffee cups on a Sunday morning of relaxation. Except that I wasn't specially relaxed and he hadn't started to be yet, although I hoped he would be soon.

"What did you arrange with Justine?"

"Nothing definite, nothing you need know about."

"Aren't you afraid she'll go straight to the police?"

"No. If she could see her way I expect she would. At the moment she can't see her way."

"She won't help you."

"Give her time."

"Ever," I said definitely.

"That's a big word."

Our eyes met. Perhaps he did feel the first gentle stir of alarm.

"Perhaps I know Justine better than you do."

"She's a lovely girl," he said. And because he said it gently, for a moment I wavered. "But I think she'll be back. She can't help herself, you see. She has to talk to me, to hear what I have to say, to try to sound the depths of what I am saying. And that gives me my chance."

Atabi got up from where he was sitting and walked between us, calling for milk.

"She's confused," he said. "The introduction of her father's name has worried her. She doesn't think I'm her father, but could I be? She thinks not. But she's asking herself: was *he* mixed up in this sort of thing? Was he a traitor? If so, where does she herself stand?"

"And was her father a traitor?"

"He played his part. I don't care for the word."

"Naturally." I was bitter.

"You knew the man, you loved him. Can *you* call him traitor?"

I was silent. I was remembering how my husband had said goodbye on the last day we had together. I think he had tried to tell me then something of his purpose in going, but I had been cross and hurt that he was going off without me and I had refused to listen.

"That's why Teddy died, really," I said. "I suppose all these years he guessed about his brother. Perhaps he even had him killed. It would have been possible for Teddy to arrange that."

"I don't know how your husband died," he said quietly. "He just disappeared. But all the evidence is that it was on the archaeological dig just as you were told."

"They were a family of brothers," I said, lost in a tunnel of dark memories. "Teddy, my husband and the eldest one whom I never met. He died before I came into the family." I thought for a moment. "Or so I believed. But perhaps he didn't. Perhaps he isn't dead at all." I looked at Stephen. "I think he is, though. I think he died quite recently. He died in the café across the way. He used the name Braun or Brun."

Stephen did not say yes or no.

"Eva killed Braun. She knew him as Braun, although of course she also knew it was a false name," I said. "I suppose that part's true. Had he been in touch with them all these years? No, I can see you're not going to answer that. I don't believe he was in touch with Teddy. I bet Teddy thought he was dead. But Eva knew because she wanted the money she could earn. She must have been very frightened to want to kill Braun. But then she *was* very frightened. I've seen Eva and I know."

"She was only interested in money. And when it comes to a crisis, money is not quite enough to hold you up."

I was interested and really wanted to know. "And what is holding you up? What gives you your strength? Is it that you have such a great belief in your country, in what you do?"

He did not answer. But even so, without words, he managed to let me understand that no, he had no great belief.

"You were all quite a good network, weren't you? And beamed straight in on me. No wonder you knew so much about me. And Anne too. You hardly needed any help she could give."

"I thought you'd forgotten Anne."

"Oh no, not forgotten. Perhaps she's got a little crowded out with all the other things I'm learning, but I know she's still there. Anne's a fanatic. I see that. I think perhaps my husband and his brother were. You could call them a chain of believers. But not you. So if it isn't your great belief in a crusade that's powered you, what has? After all, is it money?"

"Not so much of that in it," he said, with a laugh. No, he didn't look as if the living had been good. He looked thin, tired, stretched beyond his powers.

"How long have you been living, hidden among us like this? How many years?"

"Twelve years. Over that, really."

"How long since you have seen your own country?"

He laughed. "Longer even than that."

"Letters?"

"Oh yes, I get letters."

"Are you married?"

"No."

"I don't think you've been too lucky in your life," I said, not ironically, certainly with conviction.

"Nor you either."

"Your luck and my luck are mixed up together. Why did you call yourself my husband?"

"I thought it would be easier for you."

"It was a cruel thing to do."

"I believed it would make it easier for you to accept me. You wouldn't believe me but you would be willing to accept a half fiction. Pretend to be doubtful. While I stayed. I had been misinformed about your character."

"And then, too, it was a way in, wasn't it? Broke up familiar patterns for us right from the beginning, made Justine and me more vulnerable."

It was an explanation but not the whole explanation. Two can play at psychology and I thought that he had been drawn to the lie because he was lonely: he was looking for a home.

"Twelve years is a long time here," I said. A long time to be alien and secret and hidden. Unloved and unloving.

He must have read my thoughts.

"I was married once," he said. "I had a wife. She died."

"Were you with her when she died?" For some reason it mattered to me to know.

"Yes. I was there." An expression of pain crossed his face. He flexed his hands nervously. My eyes rested on the rings of scars on his wrists. He saw my gaze and covered his scars.

"How were your wrists hurt?" I asked.

"A long while ago and in another country. They hung me up by my wrists."

I was silent. He went on:

"You asked about my wife. They hung her beside me. That was how she died."

"There is only one country that could be so cruel," I whispered.

"Peasants, barbarians," he said wearily. "Heirs to no great civilisation, despoiled by the lot."

"There were an American, a Czech and a Chinese among us. We are your friends, we said, and some of us were, but it made no difference, they strung us up anyway."

"You have no great beliefs, you are not well paid, and you know you can be sacrificed. What has kept you here? What holds you?"

He thought for a long while and then said: "In the end, some loyalty just to myself."

So then, I knew that there was no hope.

Neither for him, nor for me.

I knew what I must do.

I worked fast, there was no other way, but it all went as if it had been carefully planned a long while ahead. To my surprise I was crying as I worked. It was hard work too and my hands were stinging and sore before I had finished. I surprised myself by my own strength. I was a little mad, of course. You had to be to do what I was doing. I knew this even as I worked. I was split into two people, part of me observing and horrified at the other.

The working me, of which the observer was so horrified, was moving bricks and fixing them into position with demented vigour. I was using a special fast drying cement for indoor use. And the bricks were the light kind for inner walls. They were strong though. I had been using them, you may remember, to alter my bathroom. In the summer I had been planning to enlarge my little country shack, doing the work with my own hands as many of us did. I had taken lessons in bricklaying.

And of course, what I was doing now required very little skill. I wasn't building anything really, just blocking up a door. A certain amount of moving some things out and some things in from the area behind the door had been necessary before I could start the seal-ing-up process. I had accomplished this stage speedily and efficiently. The threshold of the cupboard was a line of old grey stones which made my task easier. I covered it with a layer of fast-drying cement. I was slower over the brickwork where I had to make a double thickness, one brick behind another. I was tiring by then, but a psychologist could have suggested another reason. I could suggest it myself for that matter. I didn't like what I was doing. Understand-edly. I was mad but I was still a human being. A woman too. And in spite of sex equality and emancipa-tion and equal pay, women are still the bringers of life and less prone to kill than men.

I kept an eye on the clock; I didn't have all the time in the world. There was a bitter note to that thought, because in a little while time was going to be running with me, dragging itself out into a terrible victory.

I wanted to rest, I wanted to stop but I dare not. In the sort of work I was doing there was no stopping; it was either forward or back. I had to go forward. Within six hours of starting I had finished the whole thing. I had put the last row of bricks in. The kitchen was swept and tidy. Everything was normal. Except the blood on my hands and the great wall of brick across the closet in my kitchen.

I sat and looked at that wall. It was a huge ghastly glaring scar on the wall. Later I would paper over it. And people would say: Wasn't there once a cupboard there and I would say, yes, but I did away with it. Or they might never mention it at all. People were funny like that.

On the table in the kitchen were the tins and pro-visions I had moved out. I had moved a chair in there. I didn't know why I had moved a chair in.

Because, surely, it would be very dark in that little hole, and who would want to sit on a chair in the dark?

I had crumbled up some tablets in his coffee. It had been bitter, but he had drunk his two cups. They contained a sedative. But like so many things manufactured by my countrymen they had a slight fault; you couldn't be sure how long they would work.

Any minute now Stephen might be waking up inside the little cave where I had tumbled him. I nearly said grave.

I thought I could hear him moving now.

No, it was Atabi, jumping on to the table beside me. He gave a thin complaining cry. It was the voice of an old cat. Just yesterday he had sounded full of vigour, now he seemed old. If the worst still came to the worst and Antoinette had to look after him, perhaps she wouldn't have to do it for so long.

I got up and stood by the brick wall. I could hear a rustle of movement. I had left one brick to be put in later and I stood by this gap.

Yes, he was there.

I waited. And on the other side of the wall he waited too.

CHAPTER TWELVE

"Stephen," I said.

"Where are you? Stella, where are you?" He was moving round. I guess that, still under the influence of the drug, he was thinking he had lost his sight. I couldn't tell if he was on his feet or not.

"Here. Talking to you." I had left him lying on the floor where I had dragged him.

"Stella!" Now he was getting used to the light coming through the aperture and was moving nearer it.

"Yes, I'm here."

"I can't see you." He was still confused. I didn't answer. Soon he would understand. "Where are you?"

"The other side," I hesitated, "the other side of the wall."

"The wall?" There was silence. I could imagine what he was doing; he was feeling the bricks with his fingers. "A wall?"

"Yes. I built it."

"But a wall . . ." He still wasn't making sense to himself.

"A wall is built to keep someone in. That's right. I built it to keep you in." Tears were pouring down my face. It was nerves, of course.

"Stella," he was beginning to understand now. His hand appeared at the hole. "Stella, let me feel you."

"No." I kept well away. Tears still flooded my eyes. It was nerves, I wouldn't admit it was anything else. "I'm here. You can hear me. That's enough."

"Yes, go on, then." His voice had changed; he was back in command again.

"In the first place I must explain that the instruments to get you out of there are all on my side. There are none on yours. On the other hand I have given you water and some food. Also a torch. You will find it on the chair."

"In other words I am a prisoner?"

"Yes." Let him put it like that for the time being. There was another way of describing his situation, but he hadn't got round to it yet.

"Stella, you can't use this sort of threat on me."

I forebore to remind him that I had already done so. Now bargaining had begun, my tears had dried up.

"I suppose you'll push food to me through the hole," he said.

"You can choose your own diet."

"I do have a choice then?"

"Oh, there's a choice. There's nearly always a choice."

"Good. I'm glad to hear it," he said grimly.

"You don't sound glad."

"That's because I'm thinking that the choice is not always what one expects it to be."

"Yours is simple: leave Justine alone."

"And go free?"

"Yes."

"And if not, I suppose you imprison me here?" He sounded impatient. "Well?"

I remained silent.

"Don't be silly, Stella. You must know I can sit out any amount of this."

"You said yourself that the choice was not always what you expected."

"I wish I could see your face," he said suddenly.

I walked away from the wall and sat down at the kitchen table. The room seemed to be contracting around me.

"Stella!" he called in an urgent voice. "Are you all right?"

I controlled myself. "Yes, perfectly."

"Something's making you sick."

"No, nothing. Forget me. Concentrate on you."

"Very well then, Stella, *what* is my choice?"

"You leave Justine alone and go free. Or," I hesitated.

"Or what?"

"I wall you up here for ever," I said harshly.

There was a long silence. Then he said softly: "With you, Stella?"

"I should remain in the flat, yes," I said, thinking that I would have to remain; I could never afford to move out and let someone else move in. I would be here for ever.

"It would be a life sentence to us both," he said, even more softly.

I knew it as well as he did.

"What a relationship; permanent, fixed, lasting both our lives and unto our deaths. Bound together for ever. You tempt me, Stella."

I suppose I made an involuntary noise.

"Don't sob, Stella. Was that a sob? Anyway, don't cry for me. And supposing I accept your offer and agree to go free? Would you trust me to do that? I could come back."

"Say that again and there is no choice," I said in a hard voice.

"You're choosing too, remember, Stella. Do you want to keep me for ever and ever?"

"So you have decided?"

"There's no choice, really, Stella. Not for me. For you, perhaps. Still a choice for you."

"I give you one day to reconsider. I shall leave the last brick out for one more day."

I walked out, closing a door between him and me.

I had no idea how I was going to sit out twenty-four hours: I sat down by the window and waited for the hours to pass.

Perhaps I slept. Soon it seemed darker as if night was coming. I smoked. Some time in the course of my waiting, I found myself back at the wall, talking to him again.

"Stephen?"

"Yes?" He was alert; he hadn't slept. Was he sitting there on the chair in the dark?

"Are you ready to come out?"

"Not on your terms."

"Don't you mind if you die?"

"You'd better ask yourself if you mind if I die."

It was a double-edged weapon I held in my hand and I knew it. I stumbled away and lay down on my bed.

I spoke to him again later that night. This time his voice sounded thinner and farther away. Or perhaps the change was in me. Some things I seemed to be hearing better, like the sound of Atabi's call, but other things worse. But you can't lose your hearing like that. I knew it was all psychological.

The third time I went back to him he didn't answer me.

Shortly after this it became light and I had to accept the burden of the day. It was a Monday, a work day and very soon I should have to go out and leave the flat empty.

Except that it would never be empty again.

With my hands shaking I went back into the kitchen, picked up the last brick and said in a loud clear voice:

"The time of waiting is now over. Call out now if you want me to stop. If I don't hear anything I shall go ahead."

But I heard nothing so I plugged up the last hole in the wall. In the clear light of morning I could see that the surface of the wall was very uneven. I hadn't made a very good job of it.

I put on my coat and got ready to go to work. Then when the day was over I should have to come back, and then I should live through the evening, somehow, and then go out to work again and then back. And so on and so on.

The first week would be the worst. Here was the first hour of the first day of the first week and it was very very hard to bear.

Then the telephone rang. It was Justine.

"Stella? Oh good. I thought I might have missed you."

"I am just going out."

"You know I've got Eva's old mother with me still?"

"I'd forgotten," I said truthfully.

"She wants to go home."

"Home?" I said.

"Yes, she has got a home. Her sister still lives in the old village. She's married to a farmer. She wants to go back there."

"Let her go then."

"Yes, well." She paused. "Could you take her home for me? I don't like to trust the old girl on her own." Since I remained silent, she went on: "It wouldn't take long. Just today."

The old woman was just an excuse. She wanted me out of the house today so that she could see Stephen. No doubt they had made the arrangement yesterday. She would ring the bell and he would let her in and they would talk. Was I reading too much into the way Justine had spoken yesterday and he had answered? I thought they had wanted a chance to go on talking without me there and had come to a tacit agreement to make such an opportunity. Only I'd been too quick for them.

"No," I said, "I have to work today, Justine." And I put the receiver down.

She tried again, almost immediately, but I let the telephone ring without answering it.

There was a little tidying up to do in the kitchen before I could leave, and I busied myself with this. I didn't look at the wall.

Just as I was ready to go the front door bell rang.

After a moment's thought, I opened it. "Hello," I said without surprise.

"Hello," said George. "Glad you're here. Did you know it was me?"

"Yes," I said. "I heard your boots on the stairs."

"Oh yes." He looked down at his boots. "I'm running off."

"Today?"

"Must. I need a bit of help, though." He had come inside and shut the door for himself. "The police came and interfered with our set-up, silly things. They don't know everything, though." He was not resentful; he had kept his options open. "I'll have to hide for today. Can I stay here?" He gazed at me in utter confidence that I would not let him down.

"Are the police after you?"

He laughed.

"You can't stay here," I said. "Not today."

"Sure?"

The telephone rang again. I looked at him. You could never disguise George. From the top of his dark head to those huge boots he was himself.

"Anywhere special you're heading?" I asked.

"Just out of the city, westwards, and leave the rest to me," he said with decision. "The telephone's ringing."

"I know." I picked it up. "Justine? Yes, I've been here all the time. No, I was just busy. About the old woman. I've changed my mind. I'll take her." I listened to her surprised thanks. "And Justine. Tell her to bring all her luggage."

You see, I knew the old woman. In spite of all Eva's nagging she had never changed from her old ways. She still looked an old countrywoman, and when she had all her luggage round her with all her parcels and the packets of food she considered essential to travel she looked an old gypsy as well. George could talk by her side and be invisible. Especially if he called her Granny. I must tell him to do that. She would never hear; she was a bit deaf.

Justine brought round Eva's mother pretty smartly.

But the luggage and the parcels and the bundles were there all right. Justine had managed to get a taxi, which was clever of her as they aren't all that easy to get in this part of town. The taxi driver was so overcome by the old lady and all she had with her that he had no eyes for George and me, which suited me.

Our best way to travel was by bus. After the taxi, I got us on to a long distance bus into the country. We sat in the back row, all three together. It seemed to take a long while to get away from the city, then at last we were free of the suburbs and out into open country.

CHAPTER THIRTEEN

For George the day was like a clean slate; he could write on it what he wished. He was excited and happy. From the conventional point of view it was criminally irresponsible of me to help him run away, but I felt if he wanted to try for freedom I had to help him. I was hardly in a position to take up a conventional point of view anyway. The side of the outlawed and the lawless was mine now, too; perhaps it had been always.

Eva's mother didn't say much, she was never much of a talker, but she let fall one or two sharp comments. Fall isn't really the word though, she had them pointed like little sharp arrows.

"She was glad to get rid of me, of course."

"Who was?" We were travelling down a long straight road with trees on either side.

"Your stepdaughter. But I'm glad to go."

"Yes, I can see you would be."

"I wonder what they'll do to Eva? Well, you needn't answer. She gave me her fur coat, you know?"

"Did she?"

"Yes. More or less. That is, she left it behind for me. *She* won't want it. Not likely."

"No, poor Eva."

"Poor Eva, eh?" She gave me a sharp look. She was silent for a long time after that.

A small, very dirty, black car shot ahead of the bus and disappeared down the road. Not many people were travelling that morning. I had looked around sharply and seen no face I knew. Nor was I surprised. A Monday morning. People were at work. I should have been at work myself, but I had telephoned to say I was ill. I was ill. I suspected I was dying.

Stephen had been quite right: as his life ebbed away so would mine. Only he would be unconscious and I would be up and walking around, obliged to earn what would erroneously be called my living.

"*You* didn't want the fur coat, did you?" she said suddenly.

"Me? No." God forbid, I thought.

"I wondered. You looked a bit peaky. You have a right to it," she said judicially. "But I think I have more right."

Anyway, she had it. Evidently she appreciated it, let her keep it. Once again she fell silent.

She hadn't shown much interest in George. Or so I thought.

But presently she said: "Is the boy yours or your daughter's?"

"What?"

"Is the boy yours?" she said.

"*No.*"

"He's not Eva's." She eyed him appraisingly. "Even she couldn't manage that without telling me."

"He's an orphan. I'm just helping him."

"Oh yes?" She wasn't sarcastic, she was simply an old peasant woman and she didn't believe me. She opened her bag to get out a handkerchief and I saw she had a roll of money in it. I supposed Eva had given her this in the same manner as the fur coat. Or it could be her life savings. Her life had probably trained her to keep her money in a sock in the bed with her.

"We're here," she said, looking out of the window. "This is where we get out."

Arrival point was the small dull town called Alfold, from which she would set out to her own village. I suppose there would be a bus or something for her. Or she might even walk. Here my responsibility ended, I wouldn't have to take her any further. I needn't have brought her this far, but Justine had her motives for asking me, and I had mine in accepting, and so, it afterwards turned out, had the old lady.

She didn't hate me or anything like that, but like mother, like daughter, and money, as with Eva, was her god.

I wondered how George took our stopping point, he hadn't exactly been offered a choice, but he was already out of the bus and looking around. Apparently it suited him.

"I know here."

"That's good."

"Yep. There's a village just down the road where I've got friends."

"They live there?"

"Yes, there was a sort of tragedy in the village, I don't know what, something terrible and all the people moved out. Later my friends moved in. Hundreds of them."

George's stories always had a fanciful ring, a sort of magic touch. However, you disregarded them at your peril, because inside them was truth. I was confident that this village of friends existed and that its history was on the lines he described.

Eva's mother had assembled herself and her possessions on the pavement. She could fit most of her possessions on or around her sturdy shape and she shrugged off my help.

She hadn't quite finished talking to me. After announcing our arrival, she had gone on muttering in an undertone. Now she hoisted her last parcel and said distinctly, she wanted me to hear:

"There'll be a gentleman to meet you here."

I watched her walk away. We never met again. I saw her once, but it was hardly a social occasion and we didn't speak.

"What did she mean?" asked George.

"I don't know."

I made sure of the time of my bus back. There was only an evening bus back to the city. I had the rest of the day to fill. I was more or less sure I ought to take George back with me. I suppose this feeling was a sign that I was slowly coming back to normal. It wouldn't be easy to explain my change of mind to him.

"Let's go across here and have some coffee," I said, to keep him still with me.

Across the square from where the bus stopped was a shabby stone built hotel. Its best days were fifty years past in the era of high empire. *Then* people had come to hunt and fish. No one came now.

We entered.

"I don't think I liked that old woman," said George.

"I don't think we're meant to."

"What do you mean?"

"I mean her purpose in life isn't to like or be liked but to go on living."

He considered. "That's like me," he said. He was a clever boy; he knew his ancestry and his way forward. I was afraid he was right.

We sat and drank coffee and he ate ice cream as well; we might have been on holiday.

"No one's met you yet," said George.

"No." I looked round. The waitress who had served us our coffee came forward.

"Are you looking for the gentleman?"

"What gentleman?"

"Well, he came in earlier. He was watching for the bus."

"I don't know anyone here."

"He doesn't live here. He came in yesterday on the bus."

It wasn't true, of course. In a sense, he did live there and I had been neatly driven to this place. I think she had been paid to say to me what she did.

George looked at me with eyes bright and round, as if to say: I am innocent of all this.

"When is the next bus back?" If someone was looking for me, I preferred to depart. Perhaps she knew of another bus. You couldn't always believe country timetables.

"There's only the one; in the evening." She was a simple girl and only told the lies she was paid for.

"I'll pay for the coffee then." The holiday was over.

"Worried?" asked George.

"No. I don't believe in that man."

"Don't you? I do."

He had a shoulder bag with him and he hitched it resolutely over to the left. "One thing's certain then. I shan't push off. I don't leave you until all this is over."

"Over?"

"Well, it's only just beginning, isn't it? Can't you see that?" His was the voice of experience; he knew a beginning when he saw one.

"All right. I believe in the man."

"Yes, and what's more so did the old woman. She was the first to mention him, wasn't she? Is she a friend of yours?"

"Neutral, I'd say."

"No, she's more of a friend than you think. She was warning you."

"And how did she know?" I said sourly.

"Because she'd told him, I suppose. But that would be business."

"I believe you," I said, remembering all the money in her bag. She'd been paid.

We were standing in the cobbled square. There was a statue of the town's founder in the middle of it, a sour-faced man in a soldier's uniform. He didn't have a horse. This wasn't cavalry country round here. Foot soldiers were all the dogged squat countrymen had provided.

There was a small black car parked across the way which looked familiar to me. It could have been the black car which had passed us on the way. Surely there weren't two as dirty as that?

He himself was standing not far from the car, pretending to look in a shop window but really studying us. I couldn't help wondering how he had known how to get to us. Eva's mother had told him we were coming here and been paid for telling. But when and how had he got to her? Between the old woman and him a third unknown figure was standing. Anne? I thought it could be Anne. But I couldn't work out how.

"I see him," said George.

But equally Xandra could be the go-between. I'd exempted her from all suspicion rather too readily. After all, it had been outside *her* apartment that the man had caught up with me again.

Without my noticing it, another bus had come into the square. Now its door opened and suddenly the quiet little square was filled with people.

I had forgotten that Alfold was something of a tourist centre, that it had a history and a castle.

I was grateful to have a herd of people about us. I would hide us among them. When they moved off towards the castle, we moved too. The castle was up a cobbled lane behind the square. It looked sinister and unfriendly staring down at us as we laboured up the steep rise, not a fairy book castle at all but something oppressive and ugly. It made you believe in the reality of this type of military power.

Memories of things I had heard about the town and the castle returned to me. This had been a district torn with religious war. Here in Alfold had lived, in the seventeenth century, one of those militant dogmatic inbred Puritan sects in which the century abounded. Alfold had warred with the surrounding countryside, which remained of the older faith, and its neighbours had responded by killing as many of the men of Alfold as they could lay hands on. It was all done from the best motives, of course, we couldn't improve upon it today.

"I don't really want to go into the castle," whispered George. "It looks one of those places that's easier to get into than out of." He was pulling his hand away from me as he spoke, but I hung on to him; we must stay together.

We moved up the hill among the tourists, who accepted us without question. They were made up of different nationalities and did not seem to know each other. The man followed slowly.

"George," I said, suddenly seeing many things. *"You* led me here. You brought him."

"Not quite brought," he said. "He followed."

"It was you. Not the old woman," I persisted. "For money, George?"

He pursed his lips. "Not bribery," he said with dignity. "He assured me it was for the best. He wanted you here."

"And you too? Did he want you here?"

He shrugged.

"What makes you think he means any good to you, any more than me?" I gripped his arm; he tried to pull away. "You're staying with me. And we will both get out."

I don't know why I was so slow about realising what was happening to us, but we were in the great hall looking at the collection of armour before I saw. We had attached ourselves to a party of Germans who were talking loudly to each other and taking no notice of us at all. They were a large group. At the back of them I saw the man and I was quite sure that when I last noticed him he had been much further away. When I turned again the German group had been split into two, and the smaller unit, with us in it, was being pressed towards the door marked exit. Without being aware of what was happening all the people in it were giving way to the steady movement of the man behind. We went through the door and found ourselves in a narrow ill-lit corridor which branched to left and right. The rest of the party crowded after. There was no going back.

I hurried George forward, getting ahead of our group. At the end of the corridor I had to choose whether to go right or left. It had seemed to me that the man had shown a very slight bias towards the right. Very well, if he wanted us to go right, then we would go left.

I turned into the left corridor. It narrowed and dipped.

I stood still with George close to me. The man was not following us. This didn't reassure me as I was convinced he would move up as and when the moment arose.

The character of the passage suddenly changed. It had been sloping for some time, now it ran steeply downwards. It was dimly lit, damp and stone floored.

"This is a *tunnel*," said George. His voice shook. He was right. It was no longer a passage but a tunnel.

"We're underground."

Ahead of us I could see the passage widened into a central area. On either side dark holes suggested other entrances. In the middle was a well.

Suddenly I knew where we were. Three hundred years ago when the wars of religion raged around Alfold the inhabitants prepared their town to stand siege. From every house round the square ran underground tunnels to a stronghold beneath the castle. Here whole families huddled together while above the battle was fought out.

Ahead of us a figure moved out of the darkness.

He had come down one passage and we had come down another, to meet face to face.

At last I saw him close. He was smaller than I'd thought, big eyes, thin lips, hair cut very short. As he turned his head I saw there was a bare round patch at the back of his skull, as if he wasn't a man at all but a manikin and this was where he was hung up when not in use. No wonder Stephen had told me to look at him from behind.

He moved jerkily forward.

"I don't want to hurt you."

"You *have* hurt me. Mortally. Did you arrange for Stephen to come to me?"

"So you call him Stephen."

"I call him what I like."

"Well, what's the state of things between you?" he said.

"Men have always found me attractive," I said defiantly.

He laughed, and his laugh bounced back from the stones of the walls. He was standing by the well, which added to the resonance.

"I see you don't take the situation seriously. Let me explain it to you. I have an agent planted in your apartment. Your relationship with him is your own affair."

I was raw on that point; he saw it.

"Well, I expected it of course. Everything is going as I planned. You are already compromised. Politically, I mean. I offer you a way out. You can let your stepdaughter, Justine, hand over the information on the project she is working on and then I arrange your way out of the country."

"But the man Stephen?"

"He escapes too."

But Stephen could not escape unless I went back.

"And if I refuse?"

"You stay here, anyway, till I say otherwise."

So he didn't know about Stephen. But how could he?

"Why didn't you threaten Justine directly?"

"I *am* threatening her directly."

I moved my head to look at him more closely.

"I don't think you understand Justine at all," I said.

"There are things you don't know," he said.

"There's something *you* don't know." I still had a firm grip on George. "Keep me here and the man in my flat is as good as dead." He looked at me. "Never mind how."

"I suppose you always meant to kill him if you

could," he said in a calm voice. "I allowed for that. He was warned."

"Against this, he couldn't be."

"He'll continue to exist."

"Ah, yes, but where?"

"He can't have gone far."

"Oh, but he has. He's disappeared."

And then I stopped. He was pushing me the way he wanted me to go: in another moment I would have told him where Stephen was.

A sensitivity like mine is a weakness: it opens you too freely to the commands of the strong. This man was strong. He wanted something from me and meant to have it.

He smiled slightly: that is, his lips moved in a faint unconscious movement of pleasure. He was what my English grandma would have called "cocky". He leaned back against the well.

"A sort of punishment for him, is it?" he asked.

I saw where he had put me. If I went back, I went back to Stephen, who might be dead, was probably alive, but for whom there was no escaping. Once back in the city, I should give way sooner or later.

If I stayed here in Alfold then my hunter might well get what he wanted from Justine. I thought he was wrong to rely on which way she would jump. She was a bigger, wiser, grander person than he gave her credit for.

It was cold down there in the tunnel where the walls were damp and green. My hands were aching and torn from my labours. I thrust them into my pockets.

I moved in closer to him. "I give in," I said. "You may do what you want."

He looked at me cautiously.

"I love Stephen, you see. I can't abandon him."

"I don't quite understand you."

"No," I said dully, "but I do." I gripped the boy's arm. "I must get back. You can drive me. And the boy too."

"I can't do that."

So he too had made his arrangements to escape.

"You'll have to." I made my voice as firm as I could. "It's that or nothing."

"Then . . ." He thought for a moment. Then— "Very well." He let me see he had a gun in his pocket.

"You won't need that. Have you got any friends with you?" I was thinking of that way out for me he had been going to arrange. He would have needed more than one pair of hands.

"There may be some."

"Better tell them."

"They will know what to do," he said.

"I suppose they'll go on waiting."

He didn't answer.

I didn't speak again. It was a long drive home.

When we were nearly back, I said: "What is the information you want from Justine? Tell me. You owe me that much."

He didn't owe me anything, it wasn't that sort of relationship, but he answered.

"As far as I understand it the group she has been working with has discovered how to achieve virus reproduction outside living matter."

I just looked at him.

"Sounds dull. But in some ways it's like creating life."

"You're a scientist," I said.

"No. But I know that much. A great scientific achievement."

"That's what Stephen says."

"Unluckily with military implications."

"Germ warfare," I said bitterly. "And you want it."

"You miss the point: *we* shall publish."

"Yes. Eventually," I said. I didn't believe him, you see. How could I? I didn't trust anyone any more.

I delivered George back to his foster-parents. He did

not in the least want this, but it seemed best. They received him with open arms.

Then we went running back to my apartment.

I had to get Stephen out of his prison. What would come after that I did not know.

I hurried up the stairs. It all looked the same. Antoinette's door was closed.

My own door opened easily. Atabi slept by the window. I hurried into the kitchen.

"Stephen, Stephen, I'm back. I'm going to break the wall down. Forgive me for doing it, darling. How mad I was. We'll find a way forward. Darling. Darling. Darling."

My taciturn companion was taking it all in, including the bricks and the wall. It was some minutes before I grasped the significance of the tumble of bricks on the floor and the man-sized hole in my home-made wall.

"That was a bright idea you had," said the man ironically.

When the knocking started at my front door, I was slow to take it in. My companion said, "Open the door." He moved into the other room.

I went to answer the quiet determined tapping. Antoinette stood there.

"Thought you were back. Heard you banging about up here." She came in. "Getting noisy, aren't you? You been out in the country?" She looked at me with curiosity.

"Yes. I came back by bus."

"You *look* as though you've been out in the country."

I put my hand up to my hair. I knew how it must look.

"Really wasted that set I gave you, haven't you? You'll have to come in again."

"I'd like to do that." I hardly knew what I was saying.

She produced something from a pocket. "The gentleman asked me to give you this. Said not to give it to you until you got back. Funny way of putting it, wasn't it?"

"What gentleman?" I took the letter.

"I thought you'd know."

I looked at the letter. "Yes, I think I do. Thank you, Antoinette."

"Something's going on," observed Antoinette. "Romance?"

"Yes. It's a kind of romance. With undertones."

Perfectly at ease, Antoinette went back into her sitting room. She fed her little cat. Then she put up the dish of food to take round to her Pekinese dog which she kept at her shop. Dogs were not allowed in these apartments. In any case, she liked to keep the dog round there. There were so many occasions on which he made a good excuse.

She cut up his food with her sharpest knife. As she did this she averted her eyes. She was still a little squeamish about knives. Antoinette regretted she had stabbed the double agent. After all, how could you tell? He might have been brought round to their side again and been useful. Killing him had been a hasty and ill-considered action on her part and not, so she liked to think, typical of her. People who meant to survive (and *she* meant to survive) were cleverer. Having rebuked herself, she closed the subject for ever. After all, she had learnt something from it . . . She picked up the knife, momentarily regretting that other, lovely knife she had borrowed from Stella for cutting up vegetables for soup and afterwards used to kill. You couldn't get steel like that in this country.

'My dearest Stella', began the letter, 'you are a good planner but a bad builder. So I was out, my dear, soon after you had gone. Indeed, I can't believe that in your heart you didn't mean I should not get out. You gave me my victory, my dear, and in return I must give you yours. I can no longer continue as a spy. It is not a question of honesty, or even of a feeling of guilt (although I suppose that is there), but the wish to be a real person again. You taught me to feel that need, but I was glad to learn the lesson, my dearest. I will hand myself over to the authorities. You understand all that that means? But I somehow believe I shall survive. I shall even, in fact, reappear. If I reappear in your life again, will you welcome me? As your husband?

'I am giving this letter to your friend Antoinette; she seems a good woman. I cannot risk leaving the letter behind and have it fall into the wrong hands. One last thing; open the letter which Xandra gave you. Yes, I know she gave it to you. It was always arranged.'

He hadn't signed the letter. Perhaps he had no name he could sign to it. I sat with it in my lap, I held it in my hand, then held it to my cheek. Silly, sentimental, loving behaviour.

Then I went over to my handbag and drew out the packet which Xandra had given me. I opened it.

Inside was a passport made out in another name but with my photograph. I assume it was false, but it may not have been. Xandra had strange contacts. With the passport was a wad of currency, enough to see me out of the country.

Scrawled in Xandra's hand was one phrase: 'A way out for you if you want to take it. I have already gone. There are no strings attaching to this offer. It's all my own idea.'

Xandra, not Anne, was Stephen's contact. That this was so had been in the back of my mind ever since I had seen Xandra and Stephen in the room together. They pretended not to know each other, but there was something in their manner which belied it. Anne was the dedicated party member; she could never be a spy.

I put the passport away. I would not follow Xandra out.

But I knew there was something else I had to do. I had to go downstairs again and talk to Antoinette. She was still at home; I could hear her moving around.

She opened the door quietly to me. "Need your hair done again?" she asked, with a touch of irony.

"No, Antoinette. It's not that. You know it's not that."

"Do I?" She looked blank.

"Oh come on," I said impatiently. "Let's be open with each other."

"You'd better come in and sit down, dear, if you feel as serious as that." She led me in. I tried to study her dispassionately, wondering if I could see a new Antoinette. But try as I did the old sturdy figure and the cheerful face were those I had always known. I suppose this was Antoinette's protection really: she was all of a piece. All things considered, I took it this meant she had great self-control.

I didn't sit down and neither did she. "Maybe I'm taking a risk in talking to you," I said.

"I should think you might be," said Antoinette, half jocularly. "But not if I don't understand what you're talking about."

"I think you understand."

"Go ahead," said Antoinette in the manner of one who will listen but won't commit herself. I knew already that she hardly ever told a direct lie, but kept silent if she could not speak. She had a repertoire of phrases that allowed her to make a response without really saying anything. She had used one now.

"I want you to be my messenger." She raised her eyebrows. "I believe you can do that, Antoinette. I was surprised, you know, when you took the appearance and disappearance of a dead man so calmly. You *are* calm, Antoinette, but can anyone be that calm? That made me wonder exactly what your part was. I started to think it very likely that you were one of the group of agents trying to control me. Control is the technical word, isn't it, Antoinette?"

Naturally she didn't answer, so I went on. "It was just too much for me to accept when *you* were the one who had the letter from Stephen. I'm not even trying to believe you innocent of complicity, instead I'm going to make use of you."

"Innocent of complicity?" repeated Antoinette as if she found the phrase amusing.

"Go to your friends, Antoinette. Tell them this: I am free. I no longer consider myself bound by any agreement I may have accepted. Tell them that they cannot trust me. Tell them that I will not now, and never will be, used by them."

"I don't know why you think anyone comes and listens to me," said Antoinette, shaking her head.

"Get the message across, Antoinette. I don't mind how."

"Of course, if anyone *did* come to me and seemed willing to listen, I would try to tell them what you say."

"Yes, you do that, Antoinette. Make the message clear and bold."

"You've changed," she said, giving me a look. "I've never heard you talk like this before."

"Is it a surprise to you?"

"Yes and no," she said, after considering. "I think we're just wasting time going on with this conversation."

"I'm angry, Antoinette," I said. "Angry. Things have been done by and through me that I don't like at all."

"*You're* angry," she said.

And suddenly I saw how life was for her. I saw how each day she had to make herself afresh, to shape herself into a person who could dissemble. This dissembling puppet, who perhaps was not like the real Antoinette at all, had each day to be taken up and have life breathed into her.

Behind Antoinette I seemed to see the man I had driven a bargain with in Alfold. And behind him I imagined a whole hierarchy of people. They were operating here in Czechoslovakia, but I had no doubt their base was in London. My grandmother came from London and she described it to me. Of course, she never told me about any Englishmen like those I have met here. Perhaps she didn't know such men existed. I could imagine them (almost as if it were a film I was making) sitting together in an office in London. A London-type office with a coal fire and leather chairs. They would discuss me; they would discuss Stephen (whom, after all, they must know well. He is one of them); perhaps they would go on to discuss other projects in which they were engaged. Always in this country, of course. They are experts in espionage in middle Europe. Do they call the episode in which they embroiled me and Stephen a failure or a success? Perhaps they are above using such terms. I expect they are such professionals that they are cunning enough never to call any project a failure. "No," I can imagine them saying. "This is not a failure. Just a temporary setback. We can look to the future." Do they still look expectantly towards me? Do they think they might yet get something from me? Well, we shall see.

I don't have any sense that the relationship between me and them is over. Nor, for that matter, between me and Antoinette. I knew I must watch my step.

I still liked Antoinette. It was quite a surprise to me to recognise this.

"I won't do anything that puts you in danger," I said to her humbly.

"No." Perhaps she relaxed very very slightly.

But here in Prague we are all in danger. Our situation is such that whatever we do exposes us to risk; even doing nothing wouldn't help very much. All around us men and policies are changing and no one can tell yet how it will all end. Everyone guesses that it will go first one way, then the other, and the thing to do is to hang on. Those who survive may (it is only probable, one cannot be sure) live into a pleasanter world.

I couldn't push Antoinette off the roundabout. I might be forced off myself, but that was a different matter. I took a bet with myself that I would come through. I am tougher than I seem.

I saw I mustn't make it hard for Antoinette. "It's all right," I said. "I'll go away back upstairs now. In future I'll behave normally to you. I won't even watch your face too much as we meet on the stairs."

At the door, I paused. "You'll still do my hair for me?"

"Delighted," said Antoinette. "What about a wig? I'm getting some in."

The weeks have passed. I have not followed Xandra. She is a shining star now on another stage. I have had one or two messages. Anne I have not seen.

Justine is with me all the time. And Stephen? He is in prison, of course. He has to serve his sentence. He says it isn't too bad. Is he speaking the truth? I don't know. But he is a good man; perhaps they respect his goodness. We shall be together again, but where it will be or in what country I hardly know.

Perhaps we shall stay here. I still have Atabi and the apartment. I have my debt to pay, and so has Stephen, to this city of Prague where we have lived so long.

Still sitting in their quiet room high above the river, the older man in the neat clothes who had been questioning the other said:

"So she bested you in the end?"

"I'm not so sure," said the other. "She's still there. We have a contact close to her. One she doesn't suspect. We didn't get what we wanted. Things are hard now. But she is there, in place. She may yet prove useful. And times are changing."

"Times are changing," agreed the older man, going to the window and looking out where the Thames rolled freely past, down to the sea, to mingle at length with the waters of the Vltava.